Conni and the Exchange Student

Dagmar Hoßfeld wollte als Kind Tierärztin, Bäuerin oder Gestütsbesitzerin werden. Dass sie sich anders entschieden hat, hat sie ihrem Sohn zu verdanken: Als er ungefähr ein halbes Jahr alt war, bekam sie Lust, ein Kinderbuch zu schreiben. Sie setzte sich an den Schreibtisch – und hörte mit dem Schreiben einfach nicht mehr auf. Zum Glück! Mittlerweile sind viele wunderbare Kinder- und Jugendbücher von ihr erschienen.

Geboren wurde Dagmar Hoßfeld 1960 in Kiel. Heute lebt sie in einem kleinen Dorf zwischen Ostsee und Schlei und hat, wie sie sagt, den schönsten Beruf der Welt: Autorin.

Dagmar Hoßfeld

Conni and the Exchange Student

Ins Englische übersetzt
von Helena Ragg-Kirkby

CARLSEN

Mehr von Conni & Co:

Conni & Co

Conni & Co – Conni und der Neue

Conni & Co – Conni und die Austauschschülerin

Conni & Co – Conni, Anna und das wilde Schulfest

Conni & Co – Conni, Billi und die Mädchenbande

Conni & Co – Conni, Mandy und das große Wiedersehen

Conni & Co – Conni, Phillip und das Supermädchen

Conni & Co – Conni, Paul und die Sache mit der Freundschaft

Conni & Co – Conni, Phillip und ein Kuss im Schnee

Conni & Co – Conni, Dina und das Liebesquiz

Conni & Co – Conni, das Kleeblatt und die Pferde am Meer

Conni & Co – Conni, Dina und der Babysitterclub

Conni & Co – Conni, Mandy und das wilde Wochenende

Conni & Co – Conni, das Kleeblatt und das Wald-Camp

Weitere Reihen von Dagmar Hoßfeld im Carlsen Verlag:

Carlotta

Conni 15

Sattel, Trense, Reiterglück

MIX
Papier aus verantwortungsvollen Quellen
FSC® C083411
www.fsc.org

Veröffentlicht im Carlsen Verlag

Umschlag- und Innenillustrationen: Dorothea Tust
Lektorat: Imogen Herrad
Vokabelteil: Judith Platzek
Umschlaggestaltung: formlabor
Corporate Design Taschenbuch: bell étage
Gesetzt aus der Bembo von Dörlemann Satz, Lemförde
ISBN 978-3-551-31063-7

Mehr über Conni findest du unter: www.conni.de

Mehr über die Autorin findest du unter: www.dagmarhossfeld.de

Conni stares, transfixed, at the battered **briefcase** on the teacher's desk in front of her. It belongs to Frau Lindmann, Conni's English teacher, and there can only be one explanation for how fat it is: they will be getting their grammar tests back!

You'd need x-ray vision or, even better, telepathic powers, Conni thinks with a sigh. Then maybe you could have some **influence** on the contents of the folder.

Thinking about the test gives her butterflies in her stomach. English grammar isn't exactly her strong point. She only got a D in her last test. A high D, but a D all the same. If she hasn't done better this time …

»Conni, are you listening to me?«

Conni **starts**.

»Yes, of course I'm listening to you,« she says quickly.

»Say it in English, please,« says Frau Lindmann. She is standing in front of Conni, drumming her fingers impatiently on the desk.

---

briefcase – Aktentasche
influence – Einfluss
In Großbritannien besteht das Notensystem nicht aus Zahlen, sondern aus Buchstaben. A ist die beste Note.
to start – *hier*: zusammenzucken

Conni can feel herself turning red. Janette is giggling quietly behind her. Conni feels like **strangling** her.

»Yes, I am listening to you, Mrs Lindmann.« She emphasises each word. Then she forces a small smile and adds: *»Of course I am!«*

Frau Lindmann nods, satisfied. *»Okay, that's fine,«* she says, turning back to her class. »Before we turn our attention to your test results, I've got a surprise for you.«

Conni and Anna exchange looks. A surprise from the Dragon? Well, this will be worth hearing.

»You may know that our school has spent several years forging a friendship with a partner school in Great Britain,« says Frau Lindmann. »Some of our **Year Tens** went to Brighton in spring. Now St. Christopher's School wants to send some of its pupils here in **exchange**.«

»Great,« murmurs Phillip. »And what's that got to do with us?«

»I was just coming to that,« says Frau Lindmann. She raises an eyebrow and continues: »The **Year Elevens** at our partner school are in the middle of important exams, so they're sending a Year Seven in their place. That means they are so to speak your English parallel class. The pupils are your age. They'll come to our class and **take part in** the lessons.«

---

to strangle someone – jemanden erwürgen

exchange – *hier*: Austausch

Year Tens – Zehntklässler; Year Elevens – Elftklässler

In Großbritannien werden Kinder schon mit fünf Jahren eingeschult. Das englische Year Eleven entspricht also altersmäßig der deutschen Klasse 10, das Year Seven der Klasse 6.

to take part in something – an etwas teilnehmen

Conni, Anna, Billi and Dina stare at one another. Now, that really is a surprise!

»English exchange students,« Billi whispers excitedly to the others. »That's so cool!« Conni agrees. Whispering fills the classroom. Frau Lindmann raises her hand.

»Our guest pupils are to live with **host families** while they're here,« she says. »I've done an information sheet for your parents which explains the main points. It would be nice if some families were prepared to take in an exchange student. There are 18 pupils coming, and I hope we'll be able to find **accommodation** for all of them.«

Paul puts up his hand. He looks unhappy.

»Do they speak any German? Or do we have to speak English to them the whole time?«

»Our guest pupils have been learning German for a year,« Frau Lindmann explains. »It's true that German is optional rather than compulsory in Britain. However, I would assume that you'll be able to communicate quite well with your guests, and that you'll be able to learn a lot from one another. There's no better way to learn a language than talking to **native speakers**.« She gives the class a searching look, one hand on the clasp of her briefcase. »And so that you don't completely **show me up**, let's turn to your grammar tests. Some of you still appear **to be at loggerheads with** modal auxiliary verbs. We have a lot to discuss, *boys and girls*.«

---

host family – Gastfamilie
accommodation – Unterkunft
native speaker – Muttersprachler
to show someone up – jemanden blamieren
to be at loggerheads with something – mit etwas auf Kriegsfuß stehen

Uh-oh, thinks Conni. Now it's getting serious!
Frau Lindmann pulls a **heap** of blue exercise books from her bag and makes her way slowly up and down the rows, handing them out. She stops when she reaches Conni.
»*Very good,*« Frau Lindmann says pleasantly, putting the book on the desk. »You got **a straight B**.«
»A B?« Conni's eyes open wide. »Are you sure?«
She stares first at her book and then at her teacher, before quickly correcting herself. *»Oh, I'm sorry. I meant to say: Are you sure?«*
»*Yes, I am,*« Frau Lindmann nods. »As you know, I am not often wrong.«
»Amazing!« Conni leafs through her exercise book. And it is true. There it is, red on white: a B!
»Wow, that's fantastic!« Anna exclaims in delight. »All that **revision** paid off!«
Conni nods happily. She and Anna had revised together every afternoon until they could almost do the grammar and vocab in their sleep.
»What did you get?« she asks Anna.
Anna grins. »A B as well!«
Conni leans forward. »What about you two?« she whispers to Billi and Dina.
»A straight A,« Billi whispers back. »No mistakes, *best test*!«
Dina makes a ›C‹ shape with her fingers. »I got a C-plus,« she says with a smile.

---

heap – Stapel, Haufen
a straight B – eine glatte Zwei
revision – Wiederholung, Übung

Satisfied, Conni leans back. Fantastic, she thinks. Today seems to be our lucky day.
As she turns round, Paul and Phillip both give her a thumbs-up. It appears that the boys have good marks too. Only Janette, who sits diagonally behind Conni, screws up her mouth as if she's been sucking a lemon.
As she catches Conni's eye, she quickly looks away and **busies herself with** examining her glittery pink finger nails. Conni can't hold back a little grin of schadenfreude.
After Frau Lindmann has discussed the worst grammatical errors with the class and has written the corrections on the board, she hands out the information sheets about the school exchange.
»Read it through **at your leisure**,« she says, »and then pass the paperwork on to your parents, please. There's a **form** attached, which your parents should fill in if they would like to take in an exchange student. Completed forms need to be returned by the end of next week at the latest, please. Any more questions?«
»So when are the cute English girls coming?« Phillip pipes up. He grins. »I can hardly wait.«
Frau Lindmann frowns. »I'm quite sure that the group won't just consist of girls, Phillip,« she replies. »We haven't got a definite date yet, but it looks as if you'll just have to be patient until the start of next month.«

---

to busy oneself with something – sich mit etwas beschäftigen, sich in etwas vertiefen
at your leisure – in Ruhe
form – Formular

»And how long are they staying?« asks Dina.

»Ten days,« replies Frau Lindmann. »The English school system isn't divided into two half-years, like ours, but consists of three **terms**. Then there are holidays in between. So we have to bear this in mind when we're making our plans, as we don't want their trip to be in the holidays.« When the bell rings for the break and a couple of people hurriedly jump up, Frau Lindmann calls them back. »*One moment please!* Homework for tomorrow is correcting your tests. And you need to read Lesson 9 in your English workbooks for the day after tomorrow. That will tell you everything about the English school system. You're also very welcome to do some additional **research** in the library or on the internet and note down the main points.« She picks up her bag. »*Goodbye, boys and girls. Have a nice day.*« With her head held high, the teacher leaves the classroom.

»*Goodbye, Mrs Lindmann,*« choruses the class.

Conni grabs her breaktime snack and together with Anna, Billi and Dina pushes her way through the **crowds** and outside into the playground. The English test has become just a minor matter; far more important is the school exchange.

»I hope we'll be able to have an exchange student staying with us,« Conni says excitedly. »That would be totally brilliant.«

---

term – *hier*: Schuljahresabschnitt
research – Recherche
crowd – Menschenmenge

Anna **nods**. »Me too. I just wonder how I'm going to convince my parents.«
»The best way is to tell them that a visitor from England would be good for your English marks,« grins Billi. »You heard what the Dragon says.« She puts her nose in the air, raises her index finger, and **disguises** her voice: »There's no better way to learn a language than talking to native speakers!« Conni and Anna giggle. Only Dina remains silent.
»It's true,« she says thoughtfully. »It's a good argument. All the same, I don't think my parents will agree to it.«
»Why not?« asks Anna.
Dina um-s and ah-s before answering.
»Well, I mean,« she says. »You know we've got a pretty small **flat**. And on top of that, my mum's a nurse and works shifts. She needs her peace and quiet.«
Conni frowns. »Hmm, that's a pain. But you know what?« She nudges her friend. »If Anna, Billi and I get English students, we'll share them with you! We always do everything together anyway.«
Billi and Anna immediately nod.
»Half of my English student belongs to you,« Billi **declares** solemnly. »Promise.«
Conni scrumples up her snack wrapper and throws it in the waste paper bin. Then she and the others slowly make their way back indoors.

---

to nod – nicken
to disguise – *hier*: verstellen
flat – *hier*: Wohnung
to declare – *hier*: etwas verkünden

»Shall we meet in the library this afternoon?« Anna suggests. »We could surf the net a bit and look for information about the English school system.«

»Yes, great idea,« says Conni. »But I can't come until later, around four. I've got to make my mum a birthday present before that. I promised Jakob.«

»Four's fine,« says Anna.

Billi and Dina agree too.

Dina looks **curious**. »What are you going to make?«

»A photo calendar,« Conni reveals. »I've made twelve photos of Jakob and me. We're sticking them onto cardboard and decorating them a bit.«

»Fantastic,« says Dina. »Your mum will love it.«

»Well, I certainly hope so!« grins Conni. »But before we get started, I'll certainly try to get my mum to say yes to us having an exchange student. If she agrees, then my dad won't **object** either.«

»I'll **keep my fingers crossed**,« says Anna.

»I'll ask too,« says Dina. »Maybe my parents will agree after all.«

»Yes, you do it,« Billi says encouragingly. »It can't hurt to ask!«

Conni sighs as she **slides** into her place. »What a pain that we've still got a German lesson.«

---

curious – neugierig
to object – Einspruch erheben, Einwände machen
to keep one's fingers crossed – die Daumen drücken
to slide – rutschen, gleiten

Herr Albers enters the classroom. »I hope you don't mean that personally?« he **chuckles**.
Conni goes red. »No, of course not.«
»That's a relief.« The German teacher smiles. »Open your books please. Where did we leave off yesterday, Conni?«
»Page 64,« Conni says quickly. She opens her book: Robert Louis Stevenson's ›Treasure Island‹.
»Thank you.« Herr Albers sits himself casually on the corner of his desk. »Paul, you read please.«
As Paul reads the next **chapter** aloud, Conni lowers her head and reads along in silence.
This is fantastic, she thinks as she turns the pages. An exciting book makes the most boring lesson pass in no time at all!
She is soon so **immersed** in the pirate adventure that she stops thinking about anything else. Only when the bell goes and Herr Albers writes their homework on the board does she raise her head. She closes the book and puts it into her rucksack. As she does so, she notices Frau Lindmann's information sheets, and her heart beats slightly faster. A class of children from England – that's almost more exciting than a ship full of pirates!
She quickly stuffs her book and pencil case into her rucksack and throws it over her shoulder. She can hardly wait to get home and tell Mum the great news.

---

to chuckle – kichern, glucksen
chapter – Kapitel
immersed – versunken, vertieft

On the way home, Conni and Paul discuss how they can make the school exchange most **appealing** to their parents. Paul's sole **suggestion** is: »The best idea is just to ask them.«

Conni just looks at him. As if it were that easy!

They say goodbye and Conni is just about to wheel her bike into the garage when the neighbour's door is flung open. Jakob and Marie, Paul's little sister, come storming out.

»Where've you been, for goodness' sake?« Jakob cries. »I've been waiting for you since forever!«

Conni goes over to her brother and ruffles his hair. »You can't have been,« she laughs. »You were at school too until just now. But why are you at the Hausers'? Isn't Mum back yet?«

Frau Hauser looks round the corner. »Your mum's going to be back a bit later. She's just rung.«

»We need to put the water on for the pasta,« Jakob declares. He lowers his voice. »When are we going to make the present?«

»Later,« Conni whispers. She waves to Paul and thanks Frau Hauser. Then she rummages in her rucksack for her key.

---

appealing – anprechend, einladend
suggestion – Vorschlag

Shortly afterwards, she is standing in the kitchen with Jakob, filling the big pasta pan with water. Before she puts it on the **stove-top**, she adds a pinch of salt.
»When Mum goes for her **nap** after lunch, we'll have some peace and quiet,« she says to Jakob. »Then we can get making things, okay?«
Jakob wrinkles his nose. »Okay,« he grumbles. »But you'll have to make sure she doesn't see anything! It'll be your fault if she does!«
»Yes, I know,« laughs Conni. »Big sisters are always to blame. Come on, then, and help me chop the tomatoes.«

When Conni's mother arrives home from the local health centre where she works as a **paediatrician**, a pan of delicious tomato sauce is simmering on the hob. The pasta is already steaming in the sieve. She sniffs the air and says, astonished: »My goodness! You two have got everything ready!«
Jakob stretches proudly. »Of course we did – did you think we wouldn't? I chopped the tomatoes!«
»Thanks very much, sweethearts. I'm sorry I'm late, but it was **bedlam** at the **surgery**.« Mum gives first Jakob then Conni a kiss. »But I'm free tomorrow to make up for it!«

---

stove-top – Herdplatte
nap – Mittagsschlaf, Nickerchen
paediatrician – Kinderarzt/ärztin
bedlam – Durcheinander
surgery – *hier*: Sprechstunde

»Well, they couldn't have you working on your birthday, that's for sure!« Conni gives Jakob a **conspiratorial wink**. He winks back.

The pasta is great. Conni piles a second helping onto her plate. She's put the information about the school exchange by her mum's place. She can't possibly miss it there.

Frau Klawitter, however, just gives it a brief glance. »What's that?« she asks.

»You read it,« Conni mumbles, her mouth full of pasta.

»Can't it wait until after lunch?« Mum asks. »This pasta is incredibly delicious!«

»Do you want some more?« Jakob jumps up, but Mum waves him away. »No, thanks.« She picks up the letter. »You're getting exchange students from England?«

Conni nods excitedly. »Yes, isn't it brilliant?«

»Why?« Jakob twists his spaghetti onto his fork and shovels it noisily into his mouth. »What do they want to come here for?«

Conni frowns. How would Jakob even know what exchange students are? He is only in Year One.

»They're taking part in our lessons,« she explains. »And all the other stuff.«

»That's stupid!« Jakob shakes his head.

»It's not in the slightest bit stupid,« Mum interjects. »**Quite the reverse**.« She pushes her plate to one side and **flicks through** the papers with interest.

---

conspiratorial wink – verschwörerisches Zwinkern
quite the reverse – ganz im Gegenteil
to flick through something – etwas schnell durchblättern

Conni puts down her fork and crosses her fingers so tightly that her knuckles stand out.

»So?« she finally asks. »What do you think?«

»It's fantastic,« Mum replies. »I spent six months in France when I was at school. Then the French girl I lived with came to stay with me in Germany **in return**. We still write to one another. Claire became a really good friend. I think this kind of school exchange is great!«

Conni opens her eyes wide. Yes, of course! Mum is always talking about her French friend! And there have been all those letters from France! But she hadn't realised that the two of them had known one another since they were at school and had done a school exchange …

»So you'll agree?« she asks excitedly. »We're going to have an exchange student?«

»Hang on a minute,« says Mum. »Slow down a bit.«

»If Conni gets one, I want one too,« crows Jakob.

Conni gives him an amused look. »You're far too young for that!«

»No I'm not!«

»Yes you are!«

Mum **clutches her forehead**.

»Let's clear the table and have a little rest.« She turns to Conni. »We'll talk about it later, okay? In peace and quiet and, most importantly, when Dad's here.«

»Yes, fine,« sighs Conni. At least Mum hasn't immediately said no. That is something. And anyway, she remembers, she

---

in return – *hier*: im Gegenzug

to clutch one's forehead – sich an die Stirn fassen

and Jakob still have to sort out the birthday present. Mum gets up and is about to gather up the **crockery**. Jakob **beats her to it**.

»You go and lie on the sofa and have a look at the paper,« he says generously. »Conni and I'll put everything in the dishwasher, then we'll go upstairs and play a board game!«

»Hey, are you two up to something?« asks Mum. »Or have I got the date wrong, and it's already my birthday?«

»Wrong both times,« laughs Conni. »But you can put your feet up all the same.«

»Yes, go on! Do it,« Jakob pesters, pushing Mum towards the door. Conni rolls her eyes. Now Jakob really is **exaggerating** a bit. If he carries on, Mum will get suspicious. She surreptitiously treads on her brother's foot.

»Ow!« he immediately squawks. Conni raises her eyebrows menacingly, but Mum has already grabbed the paper and isn't paying any more attention to the two of them.

Conni loads the dishwasher at top speed. »Done!« she cries, signalling to Jakob to go on ahead of her.

Jakob grins and runs upstairs. Conni follows him soon after, but only once she's made sure that Mum is lying on the living room sofa.

One short hour later, they are **surveying** their teamwork with satisfaction. Twelve lovely photos mounted on coloured

---

crockery – Geschirr
to beat someone to something – jemandem zuvor kommen
to exaggerate – übertreiben
to survey – *hier*: betrachten

card, one for each month of the year, carefully labelled, and decorated with Jakob's colourful illustrations.

»Do you think she'll like it?« A fleck of sky-blue stands out proudly on Jakob's forehead.

»Of course she will.« Conni nods. »A home-made calendar is a brilliant present and, what's more, it's unique. You can't buy anything like this ready-made!«

The calendar really is perfect, she thinks. Brilliant!

»We just have to wrap it up now.«

She looks around her bedroom. It looks pretty chaotic after their **craft** session, but the pretty **gift-wrap** that she's bought for this purpose has to be somewhere in the mess.

Jakob pulls out a floral roll from under the desk. »Might this be what you're looking for?« he grins.

Conni grins back. »Absolutely, wise guy. So do you happen to know where the **Sellotape** is?«

As Conni kneels on the floor cutting the wrapping paper to the right size, Jakob rummages through the desk.

»Got it!« he finally announces.

Shortly afterwards, the calendar is nicely wrapped. Conni makes a couple of bows out of gift ribbon and sticks them on.

»Great,« she says. »All that's missing is the flowers. But we'll pick them tomorrow morning so that they're nice and fresh. I'll wake you up quarter of an hour before Mum gets up, okay? Then we'll have enough time.«

---

craft – Handwerk, Basteln
gift-wrap – Geschenkpapier
sellotape – Klebeband

»Okay.« Jakob chuckles to himself. »Wow, this is so cool. Mum won't believe it.«
Conni gets up and ushers her brother out of the room.
»Yes, I think so too,« she says, casting a glance at the clock. »But I've got to go now. I'm meeting Anna and the others.«

»For goodness' sake, Conni! Where on earth have you been?« Anna looks **reproachfully** at Conni. »If you had a **mobile** like every normal person nowadays, I'd have phoned you at least ten times!«
»In that case it's a good job I've not got one,« counters Conni. »It has its advantages!« She locks her bike up and grins. Since getting her own mobile for her birthday, Anna has been full of hot air. It makes everyone else feel like the last of the Neanderthals for not having one.
»Oh, don't make such a big drama about a few minutes,« she says to Anna. »I said I'd be a bit late. Where are Billi and Dina?«
»They're already upstairs, **bagging** a computer.« Anna pulls Conni into the library. The public computer terminals are on the first floor. They run up the wide staircase and round a couple of high bookshelves.
Even from a distance, Conni can hear Billi laughing.
»Is the English school system that funny?« she says, surprised.

---

reproachfully – vorwurfsvoll
mobile – Handy
to bag something – *hier*: etwas besetzen

»I don't think so.« Anna giggles. »I think Billi's good **mood** might have more to do with the people at the next computer. They're pretty special!«
Conni frowns. Special people at the next-door computer? What can Anna mean?
As they go round the corner that separates the internet terminals from the rest of the library, she sees what Anna means: two blond boys are sitting at one of the computers. They are staring at the flickering monitor, shaking with laughter as they greet Conni in passing.
»Hi, Conni,« one of them says. The other one just raises his hand briefly.
»Paul! Phillip!« Conni cries. »What are you doing here?«
»Researching for our English homework,« Phillip replies. He leans back casually. »What did you think we were up to?«
He looks so **innocent** that Conni can't help grinning.
»Hey, Conni! You're here **at last**!« Billi's face appears above the divider that separates the monitors. »Don't believe a word of it! They're just looking at **daft** video clips. You know: ›The world's greatest **blunders**‹ and stuff like that.«
Dina pushes her way up next to Billi. »We can't concentrate properly at all,« she says reproachfully. »And people are supposed to be quiet in the library!«
Paul and Phillip start snorting with laughter again. Conni frowns.

---

mood – Stimmung
innocent – unschuldig
at last – endlich
daft – bescheuert, dämlich
blunder – Fehltritt

»Have you finished yet?« she asks. »Or are you planning to spend the whole afternoon on this rubbish?«
Paul lowers his head. »Wow, you sound like my mother,« he mutters. »Don't panic, we'll be done soon.«
»Sure thing.« Phillip smiles at Conni. »Fun first, work later – isn't that right?«
»No, it's not.« Conni returns the smile. Then she turns and slides herself into the last remaining chair between Anna, Billi and Dina.
»We've already started,« says Dina. »There are some great British school sites, but unfortunately they're all in English.«
»Never mind,« says Conni. »We'll manage!«
Billi pushes herself forward slightly so that she can reach the keyboard more easily. »There are some good German school homepages too, with information about school exchanges.«
The friends are soon immersed in their work. Anna has a **writing pad** on her lap, and makes **studious** notes.
Conni casts a quick glance over the divider. Paul and Phillip are studying the homepage of the British tourist board. Phillip looks up briefly from the monitor and winks at her.
»The poor things!« Anna suddenly exclaims.
Conni turns round. »Who? What?«
Anna sets her glasses straight. »In England, children go to school when they're five years old. Did you know that?«
»No.« Conni shakes her head. »But write it down!«

---

writing pad – Schreibblock
studious – fleißig

»And they have to wear school uniform,« says Billi. »The boys wear long trousers with a white shirt, a **tie** and a dark jacket, and the girls wear white blouses with a tie and a pleated skirt.« She shudders. »Pleated skirts – yuck! Just imagine having to wear a school uniform!«
»I'd rather not,« laughs Conni, her **gaze** wandering across the screen. »It says here that most schools in Britain are ›comprehensive schools‹. And, what's more, they're open all day. Lessons start at nine o'clock and don't finish until half three in the afternoon! Wow, that must be **exhausting**.«
Anna nods, writing as she does so. »But on the other hand, the British school system is still regarded as one of the best in the world.«
Conni, Billi and Dina grin at one another. Anna sounds like a little teacher.
»What's the matter?« Anna raises her head, looking confused. Her biro is poised above her notepad.
»Oh, nothing,« laughs Billi. »You just carry on writing.«
Once they have gathered enough information, the four of them decide to reward themselves with a Coke.
»We've really earnt it,« says Conni. »Are you coming?« she asks the boys.
»What do *you* think?« Phillip gets up and stretches, as Paul logs off the terminal.

***

---

tie – Krawatte
gaze – Blick
exhausting – ermüdend, anstrengend

There are lots of people in the little library café, but they manage to grab a couple of free seats at a table by the window. Phillip brings two chairs over as well.
»Do you know yet whether you can have anyone to stay?« he asks, looking at the drinks menu.
Conni shakes her head. »My parents aren't going to decide until this evening. Cross your fingers for me.«
»My parents won't let me,« Dina says sadly. »Oh well, that's what I thought would happen.«
»Don't worry,« Billi **comforts** her. »We'll have one in any case, and you know what I said: half of my exchange student belongs to you!«
»We're having one too,« **announces** Anna.
»My parents agreed as well,« says Paul. He grins. »It'll be brilliant! I'll be able to play football against a real English person. Maybe we could even form national teams and start a football tournament and –«
Phillip **interrupts** him. »Hey, do you imagine that all English boys are interested in football? I don't think so.«
When the waitress arrives, he orders Cokes for everyone. »Anyway, we're having an exchange student, possibly even two if they're short of places to stay, my dad said.«
»Two at once?« Conni says, surprised. She knows that Phillip has been living alone with his father in a huge villa since his parents **split up**, but she can't believe that they want to have *two* English exchange students to stay!

---

to comfort someone – jemanden trösten
to announce – ankündigen
to interrupt – unterbrechen
to split up – sich trennen

»Lucky you,« murmurs Dina.
Modestly, Phillip waves her away. »We've got heaps of space in our house,« he says. »And my dad's quite liberal about that sort of thing.«
When the waitress appears with a big tray and hands out their drinks, Phillip raises his glass. The ice-cubes clink gently. »Well,« he says, looking solemn. »Here's to the English students!«

***

When Conni arrives home, Mum and Dad are sitting on the **patio**, talking. Conni sits down with them.
»We're just talking about the school exchange,« says Mum.
»Cool,« says Conni. »So?«
Dad gives her an amused look. »What do you **reckon**?«
»I'd think it was brilliant if you said yes,« Conni replies. »Frau Lindmann said that kind of school exchange is supposed to be a fantastic way to learn a foreign language. Oh, I've just remembered,« she grins broadly. »I got a B in the English grammar test!«
»That's great!« says Mum, pleased.
»Well, if you're doing so well in English grammar,« Dad says slowly, »then you don't need an exchange student **to improve** your language skills.«

---

modestly – bescheiden
patio – *hier*: Terrasse
to reckon – meinen, schätzen
to improve – verbessern

Conni stops short. That isn't what she'd intended! »That's different,« she says quickly. »You talk to an exchange student. You learn slang, conversation and stuff.«
»Conversation. Hmm …« Dad grins.
»We shouldn't **torment** her any longer,« says Mum, adding: »We're saying yes!«
»Hurrah!« Conni jumps up and leaps round the table in delight. Jakob comes round the corner.
»What's going on?« he asks suspiciously.
Paul's little sister Marie is with him.
»I bet you'll soon be visited by an English kid,« she guesses. »Paul yelled just like that when Mum and Dad said yes.«
»Really?« Jakob opens his eyes wide.
Conni hugs first Mum then Dad. She is **beaming** from ear to ear.
»You're totally fantastic,« she says breathlessly. »I'm so happy!«
»Yes, we're happy too,« says Mum. »Dad agreed immediately.«
»Of course I did,« nods Dad.
Conni **speeds** into the living room, grabs the telephone, and **dials** Anna's number as she runs. As she throws herself onto her bed, Anna answers. Conni doesn't let her speak.
»We're having one!« she yells into the receiver.

---

to torment – quälen
to beam – strahlen
to speed – flitzen
to dial – wählen

»Hey, brilliant! Congratulations!« says Anna. »Does Billi know?«
»No, I wanted to tell you first.«
»Cool,« says Anna. »See you tomorrow!«
Conni hangs up and dials Billi's number, but it is **engaged**.
»Never mind.« Conni strokes Mau, her cat, who is rubbing his head against her, purring loudly. »I'll just have to tell her tomorrow.« She puts the phone down on her bedside table and opens the top drawer.
Under a paperback, a couple of hair slides and all sorts of junk is her red and white striped diary and shell pen from her last holiday. Conni takes them both out and lies on her stomach. Mau cuddles up to her. He does hinder her writing a bit, but he is incredibly snuggly.

> This is a totally brilliant day! I'm getting an English exchange student! It might be a girl. I don't exactly know yet. But I think I'd prefer a girl. Then we can become as good friends as Mum and her French friend Claire. That would be fantastic! Anyway, **I'm over the moon**, and I can hardly wait for the English students to arrive!

---

engaged – *hier*: besetzt
to be over the moon – überglücklich sein

I hope they can speak at least some German. My English isn't that great yet. But I got a B! In English! That has to be a good sign.

Satisfied, Conni shuts her **diary**.

Oh wow, she thinks, is this exciting or what!

---

diary – Tagebuch

When the alarm goes off under her pillow the next morning, Conni initially can't work out what is going on. It is much too early to get up!
Grumpily, she stops it ringing. But then she remembers: it's Mum's birthday today! She and Jakob still have to pick some flowers and lay the breakfast table!
She quickly scrambles out of bed, yawns, and stretches. Outside the sun is shining, as she can see when she peeks through a gap in the curtains.
She **creeps on tiptoe** along the landing, and slips into Jakob's room. He is buried deep under the covers. Only his mop of hair is poking out.
»Jakob,« whispers Conni. »Wake up!«
Jakob growls and disappears even further into his cave.
»Jakob!« hisses Conni once more, slightly louder. »Wake up!«
»Whatisit?« Jakob **emerges** sleepily. He pulls a face when he sees Conni.
Conni unceremoniously pulls off his **covers**. When Jakob protests loudly, she quickly puts her hand over his mouth.

---

grumpily – mürrisch
to creep on tiptoe – auf Zehenspitzen schleichen
to emerge – *hier*: auftauchen
cover – *hier*: Bettdecke

unceremoniously – kurzerhand

With her other hand, she gesticulates wildly. »Shh!« she hisses. »You'll wake the whole house! Have you forgotten that it's Mum's birthday today?« Jakob's eyes widen. Conni pulls her hand away. »Come on, get up!«

Shortly afterwards they are tramping through the garden that is damp with dew. Mau leaps excitedly around their feet, trying to catch a fat bumble bee that is buzzing slowly from flower to flower.

»You pick a couple of those blue ones,« Conni says to Jakob. »They're Mum's favourite flowers.«

She is already holding a colourful bunch of flowers, but it still needs a little **dash** of blue.

»Perfect,« she says as Jakob passes her the flowers and she adds the **stems** to the others. Jakob sneezes in agreement. Conni crosses the patio, goes into the sitting room, and puts the flowers into a vase on the round dining table. Their present is already at Mum's place next to the birthday candle.

As Jakob lays the breakfast table, Conni fills the coffee machine in the kitchen and puts four slices of bread into the toaster. She keeps looking at the clock. Mum and Dad will be getting up any minute now.

What a shame it's not a Sunday, Conni thinks. She puts a jar of jam, the honey pot, the milk jug and sugar shaker onto a **tray**, puts the toast on a napkin, and carries everything over to the table.

---

dash – *hier*: Tupfer
stem – Stängel
tray – Tablett

Conni and Jakob have only just washed, brushed their teeth and dressed when they hear the radio alarm go off in the bedroom. Quietly, they open the bedroom door and start singing: »Happy birthday to you, happy birthday to you, happy birthday dear Mum, happy birthday to you!«

Mum sits up in bed, **delighted**. Her eyes are still small and sleepy and her hair is tousled, but she spreads out her arms and cries: »Thank you, sweethearts! Thank you very much!«

Conni, Jakob and Dad take it in turns to give her a kiss on both cheeks, and wish her a happy birthday.

When Mum is sitting at the laid table shortly afterwards, Dad hands her a big bunch of autumn roses and a brightly coloured silk scarf. Then he puts two more presents at the side of Mum's plate. Conni wonders what they might be, but Dad's face is **giving nothing away**.

»That's from us!« crows Jakob, pushing the calendar towards Mum. »Home-made!«

Intrigued, Mum feels the present. She lifts it up, shakes it, and finally unpacks it carefully. As she leafs through the calendar and sees the photos with Jakob's pictures and Conni's careful inscriptions, she is thrilled. »Thank you so much! It's a beautiful calendar! It will have pride of place!«

Then she carefully **tugs** at the ribbons on Dad's present.

»Come on!« Jakob urges. »I want to know what's in there before I have to go to school!«

---

delighted – erfreut
to give nothing away – nichts preisgeben
to tug – ziehen

Conni gives her brother a quick look. Today is Mum's birthday – which means no **nagging**, and definitely no **whining**!
»But, this is –« Mum is holding a slender silver ring with a heart-shaped amber stone.
»Does it fit?« Dad asks excitedly.
Mum puts the ring on her finger. It fits perfectly.
»It's fabulous!« she smiles.
Grinning, Dad points to the second present. »Open it!« Mum pulls the paper off. In front of her is a flat red shiny **case**.
»You wanted a new camera,« says Dad proudly.
»That's a camera?« Mum asks, frowning. She stares first at the flat case, then at Dad.
He turns a bit red. »Erm, well,« he stammers. »Well, strictly speaking, it's a camera mobile. You can take photos, phone and even listen to music!«
Mum laughs. »All at the same time? Can it by any chance iron and cook?«
»Yes, erm, no. Of course not.« Dad clears his throat. »But the salesgirl was so nice, and …«
Mum interrupts him with a kiss. »It's lovely. Thank you! It's just what I wanted!«
Dad quickly pours her a cup of coffee and spreads strawberry jam on his toast. Mum puts the bright silk scarf round her neck and looks fondly at the new amber ring on her finger,

---

to nag – nörgeln
to whine– quengeln
case – *hier*: Etui, Schachtel

while Conni and Jakob **marvel at** the tiny new mobile. Dad tries out a couple of ringtones and takes a picture of the birthday flowers.
»Cool,« says Jakob.
»Yes, it is. But all the same, we need to have breakfast now,« sighs Conni. »Otherwise we really will be late.«
»We'll have a nice **cosy** celebration this afternoon,« Mum says consolingly. »I'll bake a yummy cake.«
»And to celebrate, we'll have a barbecue this evening!« Dad announces.
»Fantastic!« Conni goes into the hall and slings her rucksack over her shoulder.
Shortly afterwards, she is pushing her bike out of the **drive** and waving to Jakob, who is walking to the local primary school with Marie.

When Conni arrives at school, there are already a couple of consent forms on the teacher's desk. She adds her form to the pile, and slides into her row. Anna and the others aren't there yet. Only Janette and her **mean mob** are there, whispering with their heads together as always.
»Hey, Conni!« Phillip chucks his rucksack across a couple of desks to the back of the room. It crashes against the wall and lies there all higgledy-piggledy.
»Hello, Phillip,« grins Conni. »So, how many English students are moving in with you?«

---

to marvel at something – über etwas staunen
cosy – gemütlich
drive – *hier*: Einfahrt
mean mob – *hier*: Zickenhaufen

Phillip shrugs. »No idea. No decisions have been made yet.«
Gradually, the others trundle in. Paul and Phillip greet one another so loudly, it is as if they haven't seen one another for days. They hide themselves away in the back row, where they begin an **animated** discussion about the current football league table.
Anna drops down onto her chair with a sigh, and rummages in her rucksack for her parents' consent form. Billi congratulates Conni. Anna has told her that Conni's parents have agreed. Only Dina sits down silently, looking sad. Conni gives her an encouraging smile.
»Good morning, boys and girls!« comes Frau Lindmann's **rasping** voice. She heaves her briefcase onto the desk. *»Please sit down.«*
»Good morning, Mrs Lindmann,« the class murmurs back. A couple of latecomers attempt to slip into their seats unnoticed. **In vain**.
»You are late,« Frau Lindmann says sternly. *»One more time, and you'll get a* ***black mark****.«*
The class grumbles. Their class teacher is notorious for being quick to hand out black marks. Fortunately, she sees the pile of letters on her desk.
»Well, then,« she says. *»I've got some exciting news for you.* I've meanwhile been given a list of names, and I can tell you

---

animated – lebhaft
rasping – rau, krächzend
in vain – vergeblich
black mark – *hier*: Eintrag

who's staying where. I'd like you, please, to write a short letter to your exchange student introducing yourself, your family, and your hobbies. I'll collect the letters tomorrow and send them off. Then our guests can start to form a picture of you.«

»What should I do?« Dina asks quietly. »We're not having an exchange student.«

A couple of other pupils whose families aren't taking part in the exchange also put their hands up. They look glum.

»Oh yes, of course.« Frau Lindmann frowns and ponders. »You write a letter introducing our class, the school, and our town,« she says. »We'll be taking our guests on a couple of days out. Maybe you could write something about the sights in the area? And you could write something about yourselves,« she adds as she sees Dina's unhappy face. »After all, you are **hosts** too.«

Dina's face brightens slightly. She smiles at Conni as she catches her eye. Of course Dina is part of it, thinks Conni. With or without an English student!

Frau Lindmann goes round handing out little pieces of paper. Excitedly, Conni takes one. It has a name and address on it: Mandy Livingston, 13A Seacove Lane, Brighton, Great Britain.

So her exchange student is called Mandy. That sounds nice, she thinks.

Anna is giggling quietly next to her. »Alisha Donovan,« she whispers to Conni. »Alisha – what a name!«

»It doesn't matter,« Conni whispers back.

---

host – Gastgeber

»My partner's called Kate McPherson,« Billi whispers to them. »Doesn't sound bad either, does she?« She grins.
Frau Lindmann gives Dina a piece of paper with the address of St Christopher's School. »I'm sure you'll think of something nice to say,« she says kindly.
Dina nods, and Conni is quite certain that she will **make a** particularly big **effort** with her letter.
At break time they all compare names and addresses of the exchange students, as if that would tell them something about them.
»Are you really getting two?« Conni asks Phillip curiously.
Phillip shakes his head. »Just one, unfortunately. Toby.«
»Mine's called Louis,« says Paul. »I hope he likes football!«
»You'd better warn him in your letter that you're not interested in anything else,« Anna **suggests**. »Then he might **have a re-think**.«
»Ha, ha,« says Paul. »That's not true! I'm interested in other things too!«
»Really?« Anna looks at him over the **edge** of her glasses. »I've never noticed.« She turns to Conni. »Do you know what you're going to write?«
Conni shakes her head. She imagines it will be pretty difficult, writing to a **complete stranger** and telling her about herself.
»Maybe we should send a photo as well,« Billi suggests.

---

to make an effort – sich Mühe geben
to suggest – vorschlagen
to have a rethink – sich etwas noch einmal überlegen
edge – Rand
complete stranger – jemand völlig Fremdes

»Yes, great idea!« says Conni. »And we can ask them to send one to us too!« All of a sudden, she can think of a whole heap of things to write to Mandy.

Straight after lunch and homework, Conni fetches her writing paper from her **drawer** and settles down at her desk. The aroma of plum tart wafts through the house. Conni sniffs with delight. Loud laughter is coming from the garden. Dad has taken the afternoon off and is **scrubbing** the barbecue with Jakob. Conni stares at the empty sheet of paper before her, trying to ignore the smell of the cake and the sound of laughter. Thoughtfully, she chews her pen. Finally, she writes:

Dear Mandy,
My name is Conni Klawitter.
I am eleven years old and
I go to the Lessing-Gymnasium.
I like pizza and ice cream.

Conni puts her pen down. What else can she write? She had so many great ideas earlier! When she hears Jakob's voice, she claps her hand to her forehead. Of course!

I have a younger brother.
His name is Jakob. My family
lives in a house with a nice garden.

---

drawer – Schublade
to scrub – schrubben

She then writes that her hobbies are swimming, reading and photography, and that she has a cat and lots of friends. Conni frowns. Is that really how you write that? Oh, whatever! It is fine for Mandy to know that her English isn't perfect yet!

> My best friends are: Anna, Billi, Dina, Paul and Phillip. You will meet them. They are in my class. I will send you a photograph with this letter. Please send me a photograph of you!
> I am very happy that you are coming to Germany! Many greetings
> from Conni.
> PS Please write back! And don't forget the photo!

Satisfied, Conni reads the letter through once more, then carefully folds it up and puts it, together with a photo that Mum has taken of her, into the **envelope**.

In her very best writing, she writes

> To Mandy Livingston from
> Conni Klawitter

---

satisfied – zufrieden
envelope – Umschlag

Before she **sticks** the envelope **down**, she decorates it with a couple of cheerful smiley faces, little flowers and a big, **radiant** sun.

When Mum calls from downstairs, Conni quickly **thrusts** the letter into her school bag together with her English book.

I hope Mandy writes back soon, she thinks, as she jumps up and dashes downstairs. And I hope she doesn't forget the photo!

---

to stick something down – etwas zukleben
radiant – strahlend
to thrust – *hier*: schieben

A week later, a sky blue airmail letter is waiting in the hall when Conni comes home from school.

To Miss Conni Klawitter

it says. Her heart starts to beat a bit faster when she sees the foreign **post mark** and the stamp that clearly shows a picture of the English queen.
Mum comes out of the kitchen. »There's post for you,« she says, smiling. »From England.«
»Yes, cool! I've seen it!« Conni drops her rucksack and grabs the letter. Hmm, it isn't exactly fat.
»Can I have the stamp?« asks Jakob.
»Yeah, fine.« Conni nods **distractedly**. »But I want to read the letter in peace and quiet first, okay?«
Jakob sticks his tongue out at her, but Conni **pays him no attention**. She slowly takes the letter into the sitting room and sits herself in the big armchair by the window.
»What does she say?« Jakob is standing by her, **craning his neck**.

---

post mark – Poststempel
distractedly – abgelenkt
to pay someone no attention – jemanden nicht beachten
to crane one's neck – den Hals recken

»I've not even opened it yet!« hisses Conni. »And I won't open it so long as you're standing there with your eyes on stalks! Haven't you ever heard of private correspondence?«
Jakob grins and drops down onto the sofa.
Conni rolls her eyes, but then turns slightly sideways and opens the envelope. A photo falls out. It shows a red-haired girl laughing happily into the camera. Next to her is a big black dog with its tongue hanging out to one side.
Full of curiosity, Conni turns the photo over. On the back it says:

> Me and my dog Harry. (He's the
> one **sticking his tongue out**!)

Conni giggles quietly. Mandy sounds pretty funny!
She unfolds the letter and starts to read.

> Lieber Conni!

Hang on a minute, thinks Conni. I hope Mandy doesn't think I'm a boy? Frowning, she carries on reading.

> Ich will mich bedanken vor Deinen
> Letter, über was ich mich sehr
> gefreut hab!

Conni grins. So Mandy's German isn't perfect either. What a relief!

---

to stick one's tongue out – die Zunge herausstrecken

Ich freuen mich schon sehr Dich zu sehen und Deine Freunden und Family zu treffen. Mein Hobbies sind Musik, Skating und Spazierengehen mit mein Hund Harry. Essen mag ich am liebsten: fish and chips, pancakes and apple crumble. Sorry, dass mein Deutsch noch nicht so gut ist. Dein English in den Brief war sehr gut, ich muss sagen! Ich habe zwei Brüder, die sind älter als ich. Mein Mutter arbeitet im Rathaus, mein Vater hat ein Werkstatt für Autos. Unser Haus ist fast am Strand von Brighton. Brighton ist eine sehr hübsche Stadt am Meer. Ich muss schließen nun, aber wir sehen uns bald!
Bis denn,
Mandy

Ps: You can keep the photo! May I keep yours?

Conni looks at the photo more closely. Mandy seems really nice. She has an open smile, and her letter sounds funny and interesting.
»Can I have the stamp now?« Jakob has crept up unnoticed, and is looking at the photo that Conni is holding.
»She's got red hair!« he squawks. »She looks like a **fire extinguisher**!«

---

fire extinguisher – Feuerlöscher

»That's just not true!« snaps Conni. She **shoves** the photo back into the envelope. »And I'll have to think about whether or not to give you the stamp now!«
She goes to see Mum in the kitchen, leaving a **sulky** Jakob behind.
»So, what does your English friend have to say?« asks Mum.
Conni reads the letter out to her. Jakob is, of course, standing at the kitchen door, listening in.
»She sounds very nice,« says Mum, washing a bunch of fresh carrots.
Conni nods and grabs a little carrot.
»Mandy's favourite foods are fish and chips, pancakes and apple crumble,« she says, crunching the carrot. »What are they? Can we make them when she's here?«
»Of course we can!« Mum immediately agrees. »Fish and chips are an English speciality: it's baked fish with chips wrapped in paper and served with vinegar.« The corners of her mouth curl up. »But you can **give** the vinegar **a miss**, and have it with mayonnaise instead. Pancakes are ›Pfannkuchen‹. We like them too. And apple crumble is, so far as I know, a kind of ›Apfelstreuselkuchen‹. I'll have to get hold of a few English recipes before Mandy gets here.«
»Fish with vinegar?« Jakob shudders. »Yuck!« He **helps himself to** a carrot too. »Can't she write properly? Her letter sounds pretty funny!«

---

to shove – schieben
sulky – *hier*: schmollend
to give something a miss – etwas weglassen
to help oneself to something – sich etwas nehmen

»You try learning English,« **retorts** Conni. »Then you'll see how difficult it is to learn another language!« She takes another carrot which crunches as she bites into it. Mum's brow furrows with amusement. »If you'd rather eat things raw,« she says, »I could save myself the bother of cooking it.« She turns to Conni. »We should probably start making up the **spare bedroom** at the weekend. It's a bit of a tip at the moment. We need to clean and tidy in there. Have you got a couple of nice posters that we could hang up?«

»Why the spare room?« Conni asks, alarmed. Out of the question! she thinks. »Mandy's sleeping in my room, of course. She's supposed to be part of the family. And anyway, it's much more cosy!«

»In your little room?« Mum asks sceptically.

»Doesn't matter where she sleeps,« says Jakob. »The main thing is that she's not in my room.«

Conni gives him a look of irritation.

Mum **ponders**. »Well, if you can make some space in your room,« she says to Conni, »so that the spare bed will fit in, then it might be possible.«

»Brilliant!« Conni turns to go. »I'll go and measure up, and then I'll work out where to put Mandy's bed!«

»And don't forget to clear a bit of space in your wardrobe for Mandy's things,« says Mum.

»Yes, of course,« says Conni. »But there's no big hurry.«

---

to retort – erwidern, entgegnen
spare bedroom – Gästezimmer
to ponder – überlegen

She takes the **tape measure** from the kitchen drawer and taps Jakob on the chest with it. »If you promise not to make any jokes about Mandy's red hair, her favourite foods and her German, you can help me.«
»But only if you give me the English stamp **in return**,« he replies promptly.
»Okay, it's a deal,« laughs Conni. »If you like, I might even teach you a bit of English. It's tough on you if you're the only member of the family who can't talk to Mandy, isn't it?«
»Oh yeah, cool!« Jakob is highly excited.
»Well then,« says Conni. *»Let's go!«*

***

Over the next few days, practically all of Conni's classmates receive letters and photos from their exchange partners. Anna proudly shows off her photo of Alisha, a very pretty, exotic-looking girl with jet-black hair and **tanned** skin.
»Her mother's from India,« says Anna. »Isn't that fantastic?«
Even Dina has a long letter from a girl called Sarah who has broken her **hip** in a riding accident so, unfortunately, can't come to Germany.
»Hey, that's brilliant!« Conni says, pleased. »Then you have at least got a **pen-pal**!«
Anna nods. »And when we go to visit them in Brighton, you can get to know Sarah in person!«

---

tape measure – Maßband
in return – im Gegenzug
tanned – gebräunt
hip – Hüfte
pen-pal – Brieffreund/in

»What makes you think we're going to Brighton?« Billi frowns. »Nobody's said anything about that!«

»Why not?« asks Anna. »Don't school exchanges work both ways?«

»Yes, of course they do,« replies Billi. »But not normally until Year Nine or Year Ten.«

As Paul and Phillip come into the classroom, the girls exchange amused looks. For the last couple of days, the two boys have been speaking nothing but English. To get in some practice, they claim.

»Hello, ladies,« Paul greets them **airily**.

»What a beautiful morning!« Phillip bows to the girls. When he stands up again, a lock of hair is falling across his forehead. He brushes it aside **nonchalantly**. *»Just as beautiful as you are!«*

Billi taps her forehead significantly, Anna giggles, and Dina's face takes on a pinkish **hue**.

The morning is almost as beautiful as we are? Conni can't help grinning.

»What's up, boys?« she asks.

Phillip pulls a photo out of his denim jacket. *»May I introduce my friend Toby from Brighton?«* he says. *»He loves cricket and French fries.«*

Conni looks at the photo. It is of a sporty-looking boy with dark hair.

---

airily – leichthin, unbekümmert
nonchalantly – lässig
hue – Schimmer, Hauch

»What is the meaning of ›French fries‹, please?« Paul looks baffled. »Fried Frenchmen?«
»*It means* ›Pommes‹,« laughs Conni. »We learnt that in Year Five! *By the way*: have you got a photo of Louis?«
»›Doch, klar!‹ Erm … *I mean: Yes, of course*!« Paul rummages laboriously in his rucksack and pulls out a photo. It is already a bit tatty and, moreover, rather **out of focus**.
»So which one is he?« asks Conni. The photograph shows an entire football team.
»Third one on the back row.« Paul stabs the fuzzy photo with his finger. »Cool, eh? He plays football too!«
»Yeah, great.« Conni hands the photo back. »Then you've at least got a shared hobby.«
When Frau Lindmann comes into the classroom, they all leap back to their seats. *»Good morning, boys and girls,«* says the Dragon, evidently in a good mood. »Only a few days until our British guests arrive. We need to talk about the excursion programme today and gather together some suggestions.«
Conni takes her notepad out of her rucksack and opens it. When Anna winks at her, she winks back. Excursion programme? That sounds exciting!
Soon the blackboard is filled with a long list of **worthwhile destinations**. The suggestions range from the swimming pool to mini golf in the park and Angelo's little ice cream shop, to the cinema, a **petting farm**, the museum in the next town, and the nature trail behind their school.

---

out of focus – unscharf
worthwhile destinations – lohnende Ziele
petting farm – Streichelzoo

»We'll never manage all that in ten days,« groans Phillip.
»It could be a bit expensive too,« Anna says.
Frau Lindmann nods. »They're just suggestions. We'll pick out two or three that are **affordable** and that don't involve travelling too far. In any case, we'll only have two mornings available as lessons have to carry on as normal and the visiting children are doing a language course in the afternoons.«
»Can't everyone just do what they like?« Janette pipes up.
Conni frowns. Typical Janette, she thinks. Always thinking only of herself. She feels sorry for her exchange student!
»No,« says Frau Lindmann. »We want to spend as much time together as possible.«
Janette **pouts**. Saskia and Ariane whisper something to her and giggle quietly.
Stupid creatures, thinks Conni to herself as she turns away. The excursions will undoubtedly be much nicer if those silly cows stay at home!

***

That evening, Conni sticks Mandy's letter and photo into her diary. She has given the envelope with the Queen stamp to Jakob. After all, he's helped her to measure her room and **shift the furniture** around without grumbling. Now there is enough space by the window for Mandy's guest bed. The little bedside table from the spare room will even just about fit next to it too.

---

affordable – bezahlbar
to pout – einen Schmollmund ziehen
to shift furniture – Möbel verrücken

Conni looks around, satisfied. She **hardly recognises** her little room: she has tidied the desk, emptied the top drawers, and added a second chair. After all, she and Mandy will have to do their homework together.

There is a **gaping hole** in the wardrobe, too.

»Perfect!« Conni says to Mau. She strokes his fur, lies down on the bed, and reaches for her diary and shell pen.

She reads Mandy's letter for at least the thousandth time before leafing through a couple more pages of her diary.

On the internet, she's managed to find some original British cooking and baking recipes and has decided to make a couple of Mandy's favourite meals with her – so long as it doesn't involve fish in paper.

Our exchange students are coming
in three days' time.
WELCOME TO GERMANY!

As Conni decorates the individual letters with a few curls and **flourishes**, she can feel the butterflies in her stomach.

Not long now, she thinks. Only a few days … She dashes downstairs and stops in front of the tall bookcase in the living room.

»Are you looking for something in particular?« Dad asks, amused.

---

to hardly recognise – kaum wiedererkennen
gaping hole – gähnendes Loch
flourishes – Schnörkel

Conni nods. »We've got that big travel guide to Europe. I was wondering if there's anything about England in it?«
Dad stands up. His **index finger** wanders along the brightly coloured **spines**. »There's sure to be,« he says, pulling out a fat book. »Here you go. Have a good **browse**.«
»Thanks!« Conni grabs the book and runs back to her room. She throws herself down on her stomach on the bed, and is soon lost in the photos and descriptions of the south of England.
She needs to know what Mandy's homeland looks like, doesn't she? If everything goes well and they get on, she might even be able to go and stay with Mandy there.
»Brighton,« Conni says to Mau. »Sounds good, doesn't it?«
Mau purrs his agreement, and shuts one eye.

---

index finger – Zeigefinger
spine – *hier*: Buchrücken
browse – Stöbern

»Can you see anything yet?« asks Anna.

»No,« Conni sighs. She turns to Billi, who is standing on a low wall, shading her eyes with her hand. She looks like a pirate on the look-out. »Can you see anything from up there?«

Billi shakes her head. »No sign of the **coach**!«

»**Rats**!« Conni looks at her watch. Half past seven already! The coach was supposed to be there at seven! »Where on earth are they?«

Dina shrugs. »They're probably stuck in traffic,« she suggests.

»I hope not,« Conni says impatiently.

The boys don't seem bothered by the waiting around. They've fished a **paper cup** out of the bin and are playing football with it in the field by the sports hall.

Red-cheeked, Jakob races around alongside them, trying to sneak the cup away from them with a couple of deft twists and turns. Typical, thinks Conni. So long as boys have something to play with, they're happy.

Mum and Dad are standing a little way off, talking to Paul's parents. Marie is hopping around them on one leg.

---

coach – Reisebus
Rats! – Mist! (*umgangssprachlich*)
paper cup – Pappbecher

She suddenly stops. »A coach is coming!« she cries.
The waiting parents all turn their heads.
Billi cranes her neck. »They're coming!« she shouts loudly, waving her arms like mad.
The boys stop their game and come trotting over. Phillip kicks the **battered** cup back into the bin.
Dina comes to stand with Anna and Conni.
And yes, it is true: a big red coach is slowly turning into the school playground, where it comes to a halt. There is a loud hissing sound as the driver switches off the engine and opens the doors.
Conni holds her breath. She looks at Anna, but Anna is looking straight ahead of her **in anticipation**.
Gradually, there is activity on the coach. Curious faces appear at the windows. A couple of girls and boys wave.
Frau Lindmann steps forward and greets a tall, grey-haired man who is first off the coach.
»On behalf of all my colleagues at the Lessing Gymnasium, I'd like to welcome you and your class, Mr Brownstone,« she says. »I trust you had a pleasant journey?«
Mr Brownstone nods and **apologises** for their lateness. »There was a **traffic jam** on the motorway,« he says with a distinct English accent.
»That must be their teacher,« Billi whispers to the others. She has left her look-out post and is balancing on the tips of her toes in order to get a better view.

---

battered – ramponiert
in anticipation – angespannt
to apologise – sich entschuldigen
traffic jam – Stau

Conni just nods.
Mr Brownstone thanks Frau Lindmann for her kind welcome and steps aside. Calls and laughter come from the coach as the first boys and girls climb out and look around curiously. A thin, very tall girl with strikingly long blonde hair stands out from all the others. Wearing big sunglasses, and carrying a tiny pink satin rucksack on her back, she looks around with an air of boredom.
Anna points to her high-heeled shoes. »How can she walk in those things without falling over?«
»No idea,« giggles Conni.
»Hello, Vicky!« screeches Janette. She throws herself at the girl and hugs her **ostentatiously**.
»Welcome to the Barbie Club!« grins Billi.
»Hey, there's Toby!« Phillip cries, pushing forward. »He looks just like in the photo!«
Conni tries to spot Mandy in the chaotic scrum. She catches a brief glimpse of a shock of red hair in the coach doorway. Is that her?
»Look! That must be Alisha!« Anna digs her elbow into Conni's side and points to a petite dark-haired girl who is looking around shyly. »I'll just go and say hello.«
Billi has also found her exchange partner, Kate, and she and her parents are saying hello.
Conni is feeling increasingly nervous. What if Mandy hasn't come? Maybe she's been taken ill just before they left? Oh no! She casts a glance to one side. A sturdy girl in a football shirt is heading for Paul and shaking his hand.

---

ostentatiously – pompös, zur Schau gestellt

»Hey, you must be Paulie, right?« she says. *»Nice to meet you!«* Paul's mouth hangs open. He stares at the girl and stammers: »Äh ... *what?*«
The girl grins broadly. *»I'm Louise,«* she says, clapping him on the shoulder. »Hast du meinen Foto nicht bekommen?«
Paul looks around helplessly. »Th-, there must be some mistake,« he stammers. *»I don't have an* Austauschschülerin, *I have an* Austauschschüler*! A boy, you understand? His name is Louis!«*
The girl starts to laugh loudly.
»Hey, du bist really funny, Paulie!« she cries. »Louis ist mein **nickname**! But mein richtiger Name ist Louise!«
»A girl?!« Paul's voice cracks. He **pulls a face** as if he had a five-headed monster in front of him. »Frau Lindmann, come over here please, quickly!«
»Hi, I'm Mandy,« a voice suddenly says next to Conni. *»You must be Conni.* Ich haben dich gleich erkennt.«
Conni whirls round. A girl is standing next to her, smiling. She has flame-coloured hair, Conni sees, and **bears a** certain **similarity** to the girl in the photo – if only it weren't for her weird hair. This mop of hair looks like a terrified hedgehog, with countless **spikes** sticking upwards.
In the girl's left ear are three silver earrings. She is wearing ripped leggings, a short skirt, and a **frayed** t-shirt that stops

---

nickname – Spitzname
to pull a face – das Gesicht verziehen
to bear similarity – Ähnlichkeit zeigen, ähnlich sein
spikes – Stacheln
frayed – ausgefranzt

above her **belly button**. On her feet are massive hiking boots.

Conni swallows. That is Mandy? A **hedgehog** with earrings and a bare **midriff**? Oh help!

»*Yes, I'm Mandy Livingston,*« the girl repeats, laughing. »Sorry, ich sehen ein bisschen anders aus als auf dem Foto, was?« Well, she can say that again! Conni swallows. »I'm sorry,« she says quickly. »*Excuse me* – I almost didn't recognise you!«

»*No problem,*« says Mandy, unfazed. »Ich hab dich gleich erkennt. Du siehst exactly aus wie in das Foto, das du mich geschickt hast. Ich bin sehr glücklich, dich endlich zu treffen!«

Conni returns Mandy's open smile. »Me too,« she says. »Hugely!«

»Wo ist dein family?« Mandy looks around curiously. »Und dein little brother?«

Conni gestures vaguely. »I last saw them somewhere over there.« She takes Mandy's hand and pulls her along. »Come on, we'll go and find them!« They won't believe their eyes! she adds silently.

Dina has been standing there silently listening the whole time, her eyes wide.

»*That's Dina,*« Conni introduces her. »*One of my best friends.*«

»*Hi Dina,*« Mandy waves to her. »*Nice to meet you!*«

---

belly button – Bauchnabel
hedgehog – Igel
midriff – Taille

»Nice to meet you too,« murmurs Dina, struggling **to keep up** with them without taking her eyes off Mandy. Conni's exchange partner is a punk, she thinks, bemused. Unbelievable!

In the meantime, a little cluster of people has gathered in front of the coach. In the middle is Paul, his face bright red. His parents are standing to his left and right, looking **baffled**.

»But it clearly said Louis in the letter,« Paul is insisting. »Not Louise! There was never any mention of a girl!«

Frau Lindmann is standing with him, trying to calm him down. »There's obviously been a misunderstanding, Paul,« she says. »Louise is your exchange partner – and she's a girl.« She holds a list out under Paul's nose and points to a name. »It says so here: Louise Wilmington, staying with the Hauser family.«

»Don't make such a fuss, Paulie,« Louise grumbles in Paul's direction. »I thought wir wollten football together spielen und fun haben.«

»It's brilliant!« **rejoices** Paul's little sister. »A girl is much cooler! You can sleep in my room, Louise!«

Conni grins as she pushes past the little group with Mandy and Dina in tow. Poor Paul! What other surprises might the English students have brought with them? She has spotted

---

to keep up – Schritt halten
baffled – verwirrt, ratlos
to make a fuss – Aufhebens machen
to rejoice – jubeln

Mum, Dad and Jakob standing slightly away from all the hurly-burly.
»Hello! We're here!« she cries from a distance. She notices the **astonished** look in her parents' eyes as they catch their first glimpse of the girl who is to be their guest. »This is Mandy!« Conni announces, unable to suppress a little giggle.
»Hi, nice to meet you, Mr and Mrs Klawitter,« Mandy says politely. She holds out her hand to Mum and then Dad. Conni's parents look at one another.
»And you must be Jakob,« Mandy says to him. *»Am I right?«*
»Yes, my name is Jakob,« Jakob replies **solemnly**, without taking his eyes off Mandy's hedgehog hair. His eyes are as big as dinner plates. »You look so cool!«
Everyone laughs. Mandy ruffles Jakob's hair.
»Thanks,« she says. »Du auch!«
»Did you have a good journey?« asks Mum.
Mandy nods. *»It was all right,«* she says, yawning. »Ganz gut, only a bisschen too long.«
Dad grins. »I'll just go and fetch your luggage.« He is about to turn away, but Mandy stops him.
»Oh, I can hol es by myself,« she says. »Ich only habe einen, wie sagt man in German? Taschenriese?«
»Taschenriese?« Dad stops.
»I think she meant ›Riesentasche‹,« Conni grins.
Mandy nods. »Yes, that's exactly was ich meine: Riesentasche! Giant's bag. What a funny word!« She laughs **merrily**

---

astonished – erstaunt
solemnly – ernst
merrily – fröhlich

and pushes her way through the crowd to the coach's **luggage compartment**. *»I'll go and get it!«* she calls back over her shoulder. *»Just a second!«*

Conni looks first at Mum, then at Dad. »So? What do you reckon?«

»She seems very nice,« Mum says **cautiously**.

»Hmm,« says Dad. »Yes, nice.«

Conni laughs and links arms with them. »You think she's a bit odd, don't you?«

»Not exactly odd.« Dad scratches his head. »It's more that I need to get used to her.«

Conni gives him a kiss. »You'll soon get used to her!«

Dad nods. »At least she'll bring a bit of colour into the house!«

Mandy has a giant, shapeless monstrosity on her back when she returns. The weight of the bag seems almost to squash her. **Groaning**, she drops it on the ground and rubs her shoulders.

»Das gehört mein großen brother,« she explains. »Daher es ist so much bigger than normal. Oops,« she gestured over Jakob's head. »Da kommt mein teacher. Hello, Mr Brownstone!«

Mr Brownstone says hello to the family and introduces himself.

»Is everything all right, Amanda?« he asks Mandy.

She grins broadly. *»Fine, thanks, Mr Brownstone.«*

---

luggage compartment – Gepäckfach
cautiously – vorsichtig
to groan – stöhnen

Frau Lindmann appears at Mr Brownstone's side. With raised eyebrows, she **scrutinises** Mandy from top to toe, and gives Conni's parents a couple of pieces of paper.
»Here are Mandy's **insurance documents**,« she says. »Medical insurance, accident insurance and so on.« She nods to Conni and Mandy. »See you tomorrow morning.«
Mandy glances at Conni. *»She's got eyes like a reptile,«* she whispers.
Conni nods. *»That's why we call her the Dragon,«* she whispers back. *»›Lindmann‹ is like ›Lindwurm‹.«* She thinks briefly, then translates: *»That's an old word for dragon.«*
Mandy laughs. *»That's cool!«*

On the way to the car, they **bump into** Billi and Anna with their exchange students. Kate and Alisha wave cheerfully to Mandy and say hello to Conni and Dina. Anna's eyes open wide.
»That's Mandy?« she whispers to Conni.
Conni nods, grinning.
Billi is really excited. »Hey, great haircut,« she says to Mandy. »Do you think spikes like that would **suit** me?«
Anna gives her an anxious sideways look. »You're not serious, are you?« she asks.
Billi shrugs. »Why not?«

---

to scrutinise – eingehend prüfen, mustern
insurance documents – Versicherungsunterlagen
to bump into someone – auf jemanden treffen
to suit someone – zu jemandem passen

»See you tomorrow morning,« Mandy says to Kate and Alisha. She adds with a wink: *»Did you know they have a dragon for a teacher?«* She giggles at her classmates' horrified expressions and carries on walking, dragging the big bag behind her. She has turned down Dad's offer to carry it to the car.

»No, danke schön, Mr Klawitter. Ich bin ein strong Mädchen!« she'd said.

When they reach the car, Dina says goodbye to them. »I'm on my bike,« she says. »It's back there. See you tomorrow!«

Conni and Mandy wave to her as Dad heaves the heavy bag into the **boot**.

On the other side of the car park is Herr Hauser's **estate car**. Conni can see Paul getting in, his face as long as a wet weekend.

Louise is sitting in the passenger seat looking extremely cheerful. When she sees Mandy, she winds the window down and calls *»Good Night, Mandy!«* right across the car park.

Mandy **bellows** a deafening *»Sleep well, Louis!«* back. She emphasises her words with a shrill whistle and a loud laugh.

Dad pulls his head in. »I need to get used to the noise level,« he murmurs.

»You'll manage it,« Mum says encouragingly. »You've got ten days.«

---

boot – *hier*: Kofferraum
estate car – Kombi
to bellow – brüllen

»Are we going home yet?« Jakob nags from the back seat. »It's already late, and I've not had my supper!«
»You're not the only one,« grumbles Dad from the passenger seat.
»Me too,« says Mandy.
Mum **engages** first **gear** and the car moves slowly away from the car park.
»No problem,« she says. »Supper's waiting for us in the oven at home!«

---

to engage a gear – einen Gang einlegen

Straight after supper, Conni and Mandy disappear into Conni's room. It is already late, and Conni is in any case keen to see how Mandy likes the sleeping arrangements.
»Well, das ist gemutlich!« says Mandy **approvingly**, dropping her bag in the middle of the room and looking round her thoughtfully. »Really gemutlich!«
»The bed by the window is yours,« says Conni. »I hope you don't mind us sharing a room. Mum thought at first that you should sleep in the spare room, but I thought that sounded kind of ›blöd‹.«
»What does ›blöd‹ mean?« Mandy frowns as she **strokes** Mau.
»Stupid, silly ... something like that,« Conni quickly explains. Boy, oh boy, she thinks with a grin. If it **carries on** like this, my English will be perfect in ten days!
On Mandy's bedside table is a vase with a little bunch of flowers. Jakob has picked them himself. Mum has put a bar of chocolate next to them, and Dad has added a children's crime story in a German/English parallel edition.
Mandy is delighted. »Sieht aus, als ob ich habe Geburtstag today! Das ist so nice! Danke schön, vielen Dankeschön!«

---

approvingly – zustimmend
to stroke – streicheln
to carry on – weitergehen

Then she yawns twice **in succession**. »Um wie viel Uhr müssen wir stehen auf tomorrow morning?«
»Half past six,« says Conni. »But we've not got any proper lessons tomorrow. So it's not *too* bad.«
Frau Lindmann had announced that they were going to spend the first day with their visitors walking through the town and showing them everything.
»We are going for a walk in the town,« she explains to Mandy. She'd specially looked up the word for ›Spaziergang‹ in the big fat dictionary that is ready to hand on the desk.
»Das klingt very gemutlich.« Mandy yawns again and rubs her eyes.
Conni, too, suddenly realises how tired she is. The excitement and long wait are **catching up with her**.
»I'll show you the ›Bad‹,« she says to Mandy. *»The bathroom,«* she adds.

A short while later, the girls are lying in bed, telling one another about their families and friends.
Mandy describes her dog, Harry, with his black coat and bright eyes, and all the tricks and stunts that has been teaching him since he was a **puppy**. Her voice becomes more and more quiet and **indistinct**, until she is just mumbling and, finally, falls silent.
When Conni looks over at her, she sees that Mandy has indeed gone to sleep. She switches the light off.

---

in succession – in Folge
to catch up with someone – jemanden einholen
puppy – Welpe
indistinct – undeutlich

»Good night,« she whispers into the darkness.
Mandy just snores gently. Sighing, Conni rolls over onto her side and pulls the covers up to her ears.
Mandy seems really nice, she thinks. Not at all **conceited** or silly. No, really nice. I think we'll have all kinds of fun together.

***

In the middle of the night, Conni awakes. Something has woken her. A noise or a voice. Listening intently, she holds her breath. Yes, there is no question about it: someone is talking!
She opens her eyes and stares into the pitch-black room. Her heart starts beating wildly when she suddenly sees a **shadow**. Conni frowns. Mandy? Her eyes gradually become used to the darkness. Yes, Mandy is standing by the window. It looks as if she is on the phone. In the pale moonlight that falls through a gap in the curtains, Conni can see that she has a mobile clamped to her ear, and is speaking into it with a **lowered** voice.
Conni can't hear a single word. She is about to say something, then thinks better of it. Maybe Mandy can't sleep and has phoned a friend? But … in the middle of the night? Mandy had phoned her parents straight after she'd arrived to tell them that she'd got there safely. There is no way she'd be ringing them after midnight to tell them that she couldn't sleep.

---

conceited – eingebildet
shadow – Schatten
lowered – *hier*: gedämpft

Hmm, very strange. Conni snuggles down deeper into her pillow and yawns silently. Well, it's Mandy's business who she phones at this time of night, she thinks. Nothing to do with me. She yawns once more and shuts her eyes again. A short while later, she is fast asleep.

***

The next morning, Conni wakes up before the alarm goes off. She gets quietly out of bed and goes into the bathroom. On the landing, she bumps into Mum. She is wearing her dressing gown and carrying a cup of coffee.
»Good morning,« she smiles. »Did you have a good sleep?«
Conni nods. »Ace! Mandy's still asleep.« No wonder, she thinks to herself. After all, she's spent half the night on the phone!
»Wake her up in a minute please,« says Mum, »so that you're not late.« She takes a sip of coffee. »Mandy can use my old bike.« She **pads off** to the bedroom to wake Dad. »You get ready quickly,« she says to Conni, »and then wake Mandy and Jakob. Breakfast in fifteen minutes!«

Jakob is considerably easier **to rouse** than Mandy, as Conni discovers shortly afterwards.
In fact her little brother is already standing at the bathroom mirror, pulling faces at himself as he brushes his teeth, but Mandy simply rolls over onto her other side and carries on snoring without a care in the world.

---

to pad off – tappen
to rouse someone – jemanden wecken

Conni is getting **desperate**. *»Wake up!«* she says. »We're going to be late!«
Mandy grunts something **unintelligible**. She fends Conni off with her hand. *»Let me sleep,«* she growls into her pillow. *»I'm so tired.«*
›Tired‹, my foot! Conni opens the curtains and lets the bright sunlight in. »Sleep's finished!« she cries. *»Time for breakfast!«*
»No, please,« wails Mandy. »It's viel zu früh!«
It's working, Conni thinks with satisfaction as the English girl soon starts hauling herself out of bed.
»Good morning,« she says to her. »Did you sleep well?«
»Morning,« she mumbles back. »Yes, danke schön. I slept well. Very gemutlich.«
»You can use the bathroom as soon as Jakob's finished,« says Conni. »There's breakfast downstairs.«
»Ich mag kein breakfast so fruh in the morning,« Mandy murmurs, shuffling barefoot round the bedroom, looking for her things. *»I'm not hungry.«*
Conni stands in the doorway. »But we always have breakfast together. Come on, hurry up! You'll enjoy it.« She is about to turn away when something else **occurs to her**. »You can use Mum's ›Rad‹. It only takes ten minutes to get to school.«
»What does ›Rad‹ mean?« Mandy runs all ten fingers through her tousled hair and frowns.

---

desperate – verzweifelt
unintelligible – unverständlichlich
to occur to someone – jemandem in den Sinn kommen

»It means ›Fahrrad‹,« says Conni. *»Bicycle in English.«*
Mandy opens her eyes wide. »Ich muss fahren die Fahrrad to school?« she asks, **horrified**. *»On a bike? Me?«*
»Erm, yes. Why not?« Conni replies **in astonishment**. »What's so bad about that? I only go on the bus in bad weather.«
»Wonderful,« wails Mandy. »Zuerst ich muss stehen auf viel zu fruh, and now ich muss auch machen Sport before school! *Are all Germans this crazy?«*
»Why crazy?« laughs Conni. »What's crazy about riding a bike in nice weather? I think it's great!«
Mandy has finally found her toothbrush. She taps herself on the forehead with it. »Just give me zehn Minuten und ich bin fit, okay?« she says. »Dann ich kann vielleicht sogar fruhstucken und Fahrrad fahren.« Shaking her head in disbelief, she pushes her way past Conni and out of the room.
Conni has to grin. What a **grump** she is in the morning!
»Good morning!« Jakob calls excitedly when he sees Mandy. But she just waves silently at him with her toothbrush and stumbles past him into the bathroom.

When Mandy still hasn't appeared for breakfast after ten minutes, Conni starts to feel nervous. She keeps looking at the clock as she fills a **poppy-seed roll** with cheese.

---

horrified – entsetzt
in astonishment – mit Erstaunen
grump – Muffel
poppy-seed roll – Mohnbrötchen

»If she doesn't come down this minute, I'll go and fetch her,« she grumbles. »Otherwise we won't get there in time. Today of all days, when we're going for our trip round the town,« she adds.

Mum and Dad exchange amused looks.

»You're often quite happy **to dawdle** before school,« says Dad.

Conni raises her eyebrows. »That's different,« she says. »It's not the same at all!«

Dad grins and disappears behind his newspaper.

At that very moment they hear banging and crashing from the stairway.

Shortly afterwards, Mandy appears with a cheerful »Good morning, guys!«

Conni almost **tips** her mug of chocolate **over** in shock. Jakob giggles. Dad, together with his newspaper, turns round in horror. Mandy is standing by the breakfast table, **beaming** as if she were trying to outshine the sun. She is wearing trainers and cut-off jeans with a tight T-shirt showing a pirate skull and crossbones. Her hair looks even more spiky than it has done the previous day. Her three earrings glint in the sun.

Conni can't believe it when Mandy sits beside her and reaches for the bread basket. Not a trace of grumpiness!

»Was für ein schöner morning!« Mandy cries. She digs Jakob in the ribs. *»Isn't it, little one?«*

---

to dawdle – trödeln
to tip something over – etwas umwerfen
to beam – strahlen

Jakob's **drink goes down the wrong way**. *»Yes, it is,«* he splutters as Mandy bangs him on the back with her hand. Mum stares wordlessly at Mandy's wrist. It looks as if she's wound several layers of **barbed wire** around it.
Mandy follows her gaze and brushes off her concerns. *»Don't worry.* It's only aufgemalt, keine echte Draht. Mach dir keine Sorgen, Mama Klawitter.«
»I think we'd better go,« Conni interrupts. »You can eat your bread roll on the way.«
Mandy frowns, then folds her bread roll in half down the middle and simply shoves it into her mouth. While she is still chewing, she chases it down with a big slurp of hot chocolate.
»I'm ready,« she says, wiping her mouth on the back of her hand. »I did tell you dass ich nicht bin very hungry im fruhen Morgen. *So, let's go!*« She stands up, ruffles Jakob's hair, and waves to Conni's Mum and Dad. *»See you later,* Familie!«
Speechless, Mum and Dad wave back.
»Bye-bye!« Jakob calls.

---

drink goes down the wrong way – sich verschlucken
barbed wire – Stacheldraht
speechless – sprachlos

Without complaint, Mandy swings herself onto Mum's bike and continues to radiate good humour. She points to her left and right, asks questions, and is amazed by the way that the cars and bikes in Germany all go on the wrong side without **constantly** having accidents.

As they ride past one of the bus stops, where a couple of waiting children are studying the timetable, Mandy laughs.

»What's that?«

Conni explains.

»What? Du meinst, auf die **timetables** stehen die Zeiten, wann die Bussen fahren? Und die Bussen kommen dann zu diesen Zeiten? Really?«

»Yes, of course,« Conni nods. »You can **rely on** it. Mostly, at any rate,« she adds.

Mandy shakes her head in disbelief. »Bei uns, we just stand and wait bis die Bus kommt. Die meiste Zeit man weiß nicht sehr genau, wann das sein wird.« She laughs. »Aber die Bussen fahren ganz oft, so dass man immer einen bekommt.«

Conni suddenly sees Paul and Louise a little way ahead of them on the cycle track.

---

constantly – ständig
timetable – *hier*: Fahrplan
to rely on something – sich auf etwas verlassen

Paul is going pretty quickly on his mountain bike. Poor Louise is evidently **struggling** to keep up with him on his old bike with no **gears**. On the last hill before school, she gives up and gets off to push.

Conni and Mandy catch up with her easily and let their bikes come to a halt.

»Guten Tag!« Louise gives them a friendly nod. »Sie beiden haben sehr schöne Fahrräder. Wo kommen Sie beiden denn her, bitte schön?«

Conni grins at Louise's funny German. Hoping that her English sounds at least a tiny bit better, she replies. *»Hello, Louise. Nice to see you. We are coming from home and we are on our way to school.«*

Mandy and Louise laugh.

»Hey, that's nice,« says Louise. *»Your English is pretty good! Much better than Paulie's,«* she adds, grinning.

»That's cool!« Conni says proudly. Just a shame the Dragon didn't hear that, she thinks to herself. My English doesn't seem to be too bad at all.

As she was when she arrived, Louise is wearing a football shirt that is much too big for her – though it is a different team from yesterday. »Arsenal F.C. London« it says on her back, along with the number 10.

How silly that Paul's being such an idiot, Conni **muses**. Just because Louise is a girl! She seems to be a huge football fan.

---

to struggle – Mühe haben, mit etwas kämpfen
gears – *hier*: Schaltung
to muse – überlegen

No doubt they'd have **heaps** to talk about. But maybe he'll calm down. After all, he has ten days **to get used to** the fact that there are girls who are mad about football too!
The bike track is levelling off, so the girls get back on to their bikes.
Mandy and Louise ride alongside one another, talking quietly in English. Conni catches the word »homesick« and frowns.
Homesick? That is odd. Neither of the girls gives the impression that they are homesick. Quite the reverse: Mandy and Louise chat and giggle nonstop, and seem completely happy!
Hmm, maybe I misheard, thinks Conni. My English really isn't so perfect yet that I understand every single word.
As they ride their bikes into the playground, keeping their eyes open for a couple of spare places in the **bike racks**, there is a loud shout: »Hey, Conni! We're over here!«
Conni whirls round and sees Anna, Billi, Dina, Alisha and Kate standing in the school car park. They are waving madly and calling: »The coach is here! Hurry up!«
Conni waves back.
»Two minutes!« she calls back. »Save us three seats!«
She quickly pushes her mountain bike into one of the free stands and locks it together with Mandy's and Louise's bikes.

---

heaps – Haufen
to get used to something – sich an etwas gewöhnen
to be homesick – Heimweh haben
bike rack – Fahrradständer

»We are late. We have to hurry,« she tells them. *»The coach is waiting for us!«*
They trot **swiftly** across the playground towards the waiting school coach.
The Dragon is standing slightly to one side with Mr Brownstone and the coach driver, and pays them no attention.
Phew, that is lucky! Conni lets out a breath of relief. The Dragon hates **unpunctuality** and can become pretty unpleasant!
Paul, Phillip and Phillip's exchange student Toby are standing by the open coach door, leaning over a Gameboy. Phillip looks up and smiles.
»Hello Conni!« he says cheerfully before giving Mandy a curious look.
»Hello Phil,« Conni replies. She nods to Toby and Paul. Paul lowers the Gameboy and stares at Mandy without saying a word.
»Wow!« Mandy whispers to Louise. »Phil ist ein hübsche boy, isn't he?«
»Yes, he is,« Louise whispers back, evidently impressed.
Conni rolls her eyes and **clambers** past the boys and onto the bus. Why does Phillip always have to have that effect on girls?
As Mandy makes her way down the narrow **aisle**, there is general whispering. Janette, Ariane and Saskia stop chattering and stare at her in disbelief.

---

swiftly – schnell, eilig
unpunctuality – Unpünktlichkeit
to clamber – klettern
aisle – Gang

Janette finds her tongue first. »Which zoo did *she* escape from?« she hisses **spitefully**.
Mandy stops in front of her and puts her hands on her hips. She screws up her eyes and snarls like a wildcat. Janette **shrinks back**, scared.
»Ich komme aus die Zoo von Brighton, du potato,« Mandy growls fiercely.
»Und sie mag es sehr zu fressen blonde girls,« Louise adds.
Conni finds it hard not to burst out laughing. Janette's face is such a picture! She quickly pushes the two English girls past her shocked schoolmates and down the aisle.
Anna, Billi, Dina, Alisha and Kate are sitting at the back, waving. Billi is jumping up and down in her seat. She has bagged the seats in front of her with rucksacks and coats. »Quick! Hurry up!« she cries. »Before the boys get here!«
Conni, Mandy and Louise squeeze their way further along the narrow aisle to the back, and drop down into the seats.
»Brilliant!« says Conni. »Thanks for saving them!«
»No problem,« grins Billi. *»You're welcome!«*
The coach is practically full. Mandy and Louise wave to their classmates and respond to a couple of shouts. Conni doesn't understand a word.
Amazing, she thinks. Is that how they feel when we talk German to one another?
She can see Phillip, Paul and Toby squeezing into the last few seats further forward. Paul doesn't seem to think it in the

---

spitefully – gehässig
to shrink back – zurückschrecken

slightest bit necessary to look after his guest! Never mind, thinks Conni. Then we'll look after Louise instead.

Frau Lindmann and Mr Brownstone go slowly along the rows, counting heads.

»Ah, so our **stragglers** are here as well!« says their teacher to Conni, Mandy and Louise. *»Good morning, girls.«*

»Good morning, Mrs Lindmann,« the three **chorus**. The Dragon hands Mandy and Louise two little cards in see-through **plastic covers**.

»These are your **student ID cards**,« she explains. »They'll give you reduced-price entry to the swimming pool and the cinema, and you can use them to buy a weekly bus ticket. They're already filled in and stamped. You just have to sign them. Please don't lose them.« She turns and goes back to the front.

Full of curiosity, Mandy and Louise turn their ID cards round and round in their hands.

»Look at that,« says Louise in awe. *»A genuine German passport!«*

»That's cool,« Mandy says, looking impressed. »And I can use it für alles and überall?«

»Yes, almost,« Conni replies. *»You only have to* … Rats!« she interrupts herself. »Do any of you happen to know what ›unterschreiben‹ is in English?« she asks her friends.

»No,« says Anna.

---

straggler – Nachzügler
to chorus – etwas im Chor sagen
plastic cover – Plastikhülle
student ID card – Schülerausweis

»Me neither,« murmurs Dina.
»To sign!« Billi cries. *»You have to sign it!«*
They all laugh.
»Okay!« With a triumphant gesture, Mandy pulls out a biro. *»Let's do it!«*

A short while later, the coach is pulling out of the Lessing Gymnasium car park. Conni relaxes and leans back.
This is a hundred times better than school, she thinks with satisfaction. No, a thousand times better!
Anna is staring the whole time at the back of Mandy's spiky head. She leans forwards and whispers to Conni: »Hey, what's she like?«
»Totally brilliant,« Conni whispers back.
»But she looks so … so different,« Anna murmurs. »Everyone's staring at her.«
»So what?« Conni hisses. »Whatever. Mandy's the way she is. Her clothes and the way she looks are just on the outside. Alisha looks a bit different from us too, doesn't she?«
Anna **retreats**. »That's true,« she says thoughtfully. »You're right.«
Frau Lindmann uses the short journey to point out the town's few sights.
The exchange students look curiously out of the windows, turning their heads this way and that so as not to miss anything.
»Look at that!« Mandy keeps saying. *»That's so nice!«*

---

to retreat – sich zurückziehen, zurücklehnen

She has pulled a **single-use camera** out of her bag and is snapping what seems to be every single building and every other tree that they pass. Along with practically every dog that **bears** even the tiniest **similarity** to her Harry.
Conni has kindly given Mandy the window seat, and is amazed by how excited Mandy is. She herself thinks it a bit boring, driving through a town that she **knows like the back of her hand**. All the same, she pricks up her ears when Frau Lindmann reaches for the microphone and, like a tourist guide, points out the most important places that they are passing: the old Town Hall and market place, the statue of some poet or other, the library …
Frau Lindmann has something to say about every single building – and in English!
When the coach finally stops, Frau Lindmann asks once more for their attention. »You can go and **investigate** the town on your own now. Get yourselves into small groups and stay together. We'll meet in two hours' time back here.«
»Brilliant!« says Conni. She and the others push their way into the fresh air. Outside, they stop and stretch.
»My ›Hintern‹ has gone **numb** from all that sitting,« moans Anna.

---

single-use camera – Einwegkamera
to bear similarity to someone/something – jemandem/etwas ähnlich sehen
to know something like the back of one's hand – etwas in- und auswendig kennen
to investigate something – *hier*: etwas erkunden
numb – taub

Alisha frowns. »What does ›Hintern‹ mean?« she asks interestedly.
Anna's cheeks turn slightly pink. *»I'm sorry,«* she says, *»but I don't know the English word for it.«*
Billi **comes to her rescue**. *»Bottom, backside, behind,«* the words shoot out of her. She grins and demonstratively **waggles** her bottom.
Alisha laughs. *»Ah, I see!* Danke, your English is nearly perfect!«
»Not at all,« Billi replies modestly. »Überhaupt nicht.«
»Und, what are we going to do with unsere freie Zeit nun?« Kate interrupts. She looks around **expectantly**.
»Wir machen einen Stadtbummel!« says Billi, before translating: *»We are going for a stroll.«*
»What about going to Angelo's for an ice cream first?« Conni suggests. »I'd love a chocolate sundae with whipped cream and ›Streuseln‹!«
»At this time of day?« Anna takes off her glasses and polishes them on the hem of her t-shirt. »I've only just had breakfast!«
»So what?« says Conni. »Ice cream is tasty at any time of day!«
»Oh yes!« Dina says enthusiastically.
»Great idea!« cries Mandy. »Ich liebe ice cream! Aber was ist ›Streuseln‹?«
»I will show you,« says Conni. *»Just wait and see!«*

---

to come to someone's rescue – jemandem zur Hilfe kommen
to waggle – wackeln, wedeln
expectantly – erwartungsvoll

Cheerfully, they make their way to the little **ice cream parlour** which – as Dina firmly insists – is said to offer more than forty different kinds of ice cream.
»Rubbish,« says Anna. »There aren't even that many different flavours!«
Dina shrugs. »We'll see.«
As they pass a **chemist's**, the English girls stop for a rummage in the baskets outside the door.
»Hey! Look was ich habe gefunden!« Mandy cries. She is holding up a little pink tub. *»Raspberry lip gloss!«*
Raspberry lip gloss? Conni pulls a face. She has found a couple of reduced-price hair bobbles with funny stripes and goes into the shop to pay for them. Mandy follows her with the tub of lip gloss.
Anna asks at the counter for some free **samples**. The assistant nods kindly and fills a plastic bag with a variety of perfume and cream samples.
»That was really nice of her,« says Dina once they are back outside, examining Anna's **loot**.
»You can all choose something,« Anna says generously.
The goodies are shared out in a trice.
Mandy raises her hand. »And what about our Eiskrem mit Streuseln?«
Conni laughs. »Hey, Mandy, your German's getting better and better! Come on, off we go!« she cries, running off. »See who gets there first!«

---

ice cream parlour – Eisdiele
chemist's – Drogerie
samples – Proben
loot – Beute

The others don't need telling twice. Laughing, they race into the pedestrian precinct and, out of breath, arrive in the market place at the little café that, with its gaily striped awning, attractive wicker tables and matching chairs, invites people to sit outside.

Panting, the girls drop down onto the chairs. At the next table, three old ladies put their heads together and look suspiciously at Mandy, but she doesn't seem to notice. She stretches out her legs and yawns widely.

»Look, you lot,« Dina says, pointing to a big sign. »Forty different types of ice cream!«

»Incredible,« says Anna. »You don't know where to start!«

»I'm sticking to my **chocolate sundae**,« says Conni. »With ›Streuseln‹, of course,« she adds.

»Das nehm ich auch,« says Mandy. »I want to try German Streuseln!«

When the waitress arrives, Conni orders two large chocolate sundaes. Anna, Billi, Kate and Alisha order the exotic version with tropical fruits and cream. Dina and Louise are **bold** and order one of the newest creations: **elderberry**, peppermint and kiwi ice cream with **liquorice** ›Streuseln‹ – or ›sprinkles‹.

»Liquorice sprinkles?« Anna's glasses almost slide off her nose.

Dina giggles. »Why not? It's something different!«

---

chocolate sundae – Schokoladeneisbecher
bold – mutig
elderberry – Holunder
liquorice – Lakritz

»You can say that again!« Billi shudders.

Mandy leans back and blinks in the warm autumn sun. »Wann müssen wir go back to the Bus?« she asks sleepily.

Anna looks at her watch. »We've got almost a whole hour left.«

»That's wunderbar,« murmurs Mandy. »Und so gemutlich!«

Conni smiles dreamily. Sunshine and ice cream instead of school and homework, she thinks as she shovels a mountain of cream into her mouth and lets it melt on her tongue. *Oh ja, that is really wunderbar*!

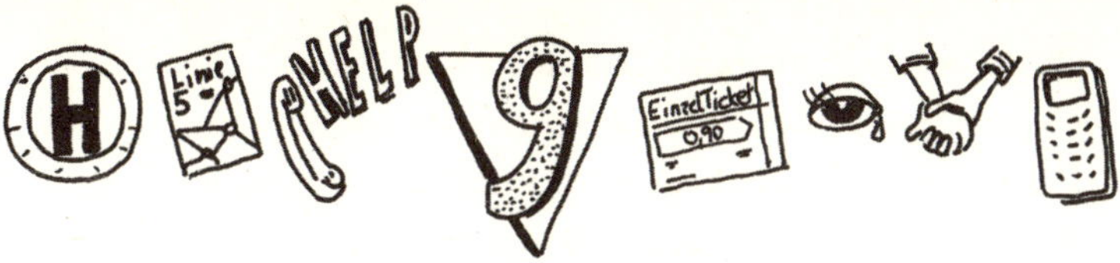

That afternoon, Mandy and her class have a German course at a language school in town. Dad is going to drive her there in the car after lunch.

»That fits in fine,« he says. »I've got a meeting very close to the school.«

»But how's she going to get back?« Mum asks. »I've got to go straight back to the surgery. My afternoon's **chock-a-block**.«

»Das ist überhaupt no problem,« Mandy says cheerfully. »Ich nehm die Bus. Ich mag es, in deutsche Bussen zu fahren. Sie sind so gemutlich, you know!«

Conni nods and grins.

Mum shakes her head. »I'm not sure, Mandy,« she says **hesitantly**. »On the bus on your own? You really don't know your way round yet.«

Conni jumps up and fetches the timetable. »Oh, she'll manage it,« she says firmly. »She's not **daft**!«

Mandy glances at her gratefully.

»The bus stop is right outside the language school.« Conni shows Mandy the back of the timetable, which shows the **in-**

---

chock-a-block – rappelvoll, proppenvoll
hesitantly – zögernd
daft – blöd

dividual stops. »Here, see? You take the number 5, then nothing can go wrong. You get on at the school and go for six stops. You just have to make sure you get off at the right time. When does the language course finish?«
»About half past three.«
»Right, then you're best off catching the bus at twenty to.« With a pencil, Conni puts a cross by the bus stop on the timetable and underlines the departure time. »It takes about twenty minutes to get to ours. I'll meet you here at the bus stop, okay?« She draws a fat cross at the stop where Mandy has to get off. »You'll see me waiting there.«
»Okay,« Mandy murmurs. »Ich schaffe das!«
»Of course you will,« says Conni. *»There's no doubt about it!«*
»Eh?« Jakob frowns. »What does that mean?«
»Daran besteht kein Zweifel,« say Conni and Mandy as if with one voice. They look at one another and laugh.
»No doubts at all,« Conni adds, grinning. »Keinerlei Zweifel!«

That afternoon, Conni finds herself completely alone. Dad and Mandy are on their way into town; Mum is working at the children's clinic; and Jakob is at his **gym class**. The house is unusually silent and empty.
In order to have at least something to do, Conni washes up the dishes, re-fills Mau's bowl, and even sorts the magazines for the **recycling collection**.

---

individual – *hier*: einzeln
gym class – Turnen
recycling collection – Altpapiersammlung

She is terribly bored, and realises that it is really very **dreary** without Mandy and her lively, cheerful manner. Even Mau slinks around the house as if he were missing Mandy. Conni is just wondering whether she shouldn't ring Anna, Billi or Dina when she remembers that her friends have already made plans: Anna has her riding lesson, Billi has said that she has to go to the dentist, and Dina is at the school art club.
Oh great! Conni sighs once more. So she is facing a long, dreary, lonely afternoon.
Feeling bad-tempered, she goes up to her room and looks around. Mandy seems to be not only a morning grump, but a real **slob**: her things are scattered everywhere. You can hardly even see the **carpet**!
Conni picks her way through the clothes that are lying around, and throws herself onto the bed. Then she takes her diary from her bedside drawer and flicks through it a bit.
When she sees the photo of Mandy, she has to laugh. She looks completely normal in it – not a trace of punky hair! She turns over a new page and starts to write:

> The English students have been
> here for a day and a night already.
> **Hang on!** You have to say »the British
> students«, according to the Dragon.
> Mandy is really lovely. I feel as if
> I've know her for ages. Weird, eh?

---

dreary – eintönig, langweilig
slob – Chaot
carpet – Teppich
hang on – Moment

I don't know anything about her except that she's called Mandy, she's the same age as me, and she has a dog called Harry. Although her German is almost even worse than my English (believe it or not!), we get on really well and have (almost) no problems understanding one another.
We went into town today with the exchange class. We were really supposed to be showing our Engli... – sorry! – British exchange students all the sights. But we had a nice ice cream instead. ☺
Paul isn't **bothering with** Louise at all. I think it's really stupid of him, but he **presumably** hasn't got over the shock of being the only boy to get a GIRL! Ha ha, never mind. We'll look after Louise. That way, Dina gets an exchange student too. I think, though, that Louise would actually much prefer playing football with Paul and the other boys.

---

to bother with someone/something – *hier*: sich um jemanden/etwas kümmern
presumably – wahrscheinlich

Conni looks at the time. Already just gone half past three. So Mandy's language course must have finished by now.
She puts her pen and diary back in her drawer and fetches out a little crystal ball.
When Conni holds it up to the light, a ray of sunlight shines into it and makes the glass **sparkle** with all the colours of the rainbow.
Conni smiles. She'd found the ball in a dark forest one night. She'd got lost and hadn't been able to find her way back to their camp. But Phillip had looked for her and found her and –
Ring, ring! The sound of the phone **jerks her from** her dreams.
Two stairs at a time, she races downstairs and answers it. »Hello? Conni Klawitter here.«
A quiet sobbing comes down the **receiver**.
»Hello?« Conni says again. »Who's that?«
»It's me …,« someone **sobs**. *»Help me, Conni … please, help me … It's urgent! I need your help, Conni! Please come and get me out of here!«*
»Mandy?« Conni asks, concerned. »Is it you? Has something happened?« She is clutching the receiver so tightly that her knuckles are white. »Mandy! Say something!«
She hears loud snuffling and a nose being blown noisily, then a trembling voice says: *»I'm in trouble. I don't know what*

---

to sparkle – funkeln
to jerk someone from something – jemanden aus etwas herausreißen
receiver – Hörer
to sob – schluchzen

to do. I don't understand a word. Please, Conni, you have to help me!«

»Hang on a minute, calm down,« says Conni. She is quite sure now that it is Mandy on the phone. But what has happened to her? She sounds so terribly upset!

Conni takes a deep breath, then counts slowly to ten and asks calmly: »What's wrong, Mandy? Where are you? Did you miss the bus? Have you had an accident?«

From the other end of the receiver comes only a soft whimpering sound.

Conni madly searches for the right words.

»What happened, Mandy?« she asks urgently. *»Where are you? Did you miss the bus? Are you hurt?«*

»*No, I'm not hurt.* Ich war in die Bus,« sniffs Mandy. »Aber dann two men came and asked me to –«

»Two men?« Conni interrupts. Her words are tripping over each other. »What kind of men?«

»I don't know,« Mandy says quietly. *»They wanted to see my ticket.«*

»Your ›*ticket*‹?« Conni **knits her eyebrows**. »Oh!« she says, banging herself on the forehead with the palm of her hand. »You mean your *Fahrkarte*!«

»Yes, yes!« Mandy says, all **agitated**. *»That's what they said:* ›Die Fahrkarte, bitte!‹«

»So?« Conni rubs her nose. A **ticket inspector** is absolutely no reason to become hysterical!

---

to knit one's eyebrows – die Augenbrauen zusammenziehen
agitated – aufgeregt, aufgewühlt
ticket inspector – Fahrkartenkontrolleur

»But I didn't have a Fahrkarte!« Mandy cries down the phone.
Conni is taken aback. »Why on earth not?« she asks. »I told you that you had to buy a ticket from the bus driver!«
»Ich habe das vergessen,« Mandy mumbles. »I showed them mein Schülerausweis anstatt die Fahrkarte.«
Conni swallows.
»Conni? Are you still there?« Mandy says.
»Yes,« Conni says quickly. »I'm still here. Hang on a minute … you showed the ticket inspectors your student ID card instead of a bus ticket?«
»Erm, yes, I think so …« Mandy clears her throat.
Oh dear! Mandy has been caught **fare-dodging**! Conni leans against the wall and briefly shuts her eyes. Oh, that is just great!
»Where are you now?« she asks slowly.
»At the Busbüro an die Bahnhof,« replies Mandy. »They say ich kann nicht gehen, bevor ich bezahle den Strafgeld.«
Conni tries to sound **confident**. »Don't worry, Mandy. I'll call Mum and Dad, and then we'll come and collect you, okay?«
»You'll come and get me out of here?« Mandy breathes an audible sigh of relief. *»But please hurry!«*
»Yes, we'll hurry,« Conni promises. »We'll be with you in ten minutes. *Ten minutes, okay?*«
Mandy whispers: »Don't forget das money!«

---

fare-dodging – Schwarzfahren
confident – *hier*: zuversichtlich

Although she doesn't feel like it, Conni can't help grinning. »Yes, okay. We'll bring enough money with us. See you soon! *Don't worry*!«

She hangs up and immediately **dials** Dad's work number.

Oh my goodness! she thinks, as she hears the dialling tone. This is just unbelievable!

Dad's colleague answers. »Hello, Conni. No, I'm sorry, your father has got a meeting in the building control department. I'm not expecting him back before six. Would you like me to pass on a message?«

»No thanks. I'll try him again later.« Conni puts the phone down. Rats! She rings Mum at the surgery. **Engaged**! She seems **to be jinxed**! Her gaze wanders across the little low cupboard in the hall, and stops at Mum's old mobile and the wallet of emergency money.

Conni chews her bottom lip thoughtfully.

In the wallet there are always two ten-euro notes and some change – for emergencies. In case the man comes to deliver drinks when Mum and Dad aren't in. Or in case the postman needs money for a cash-on-delivery parcel.

The old mobile is switched on and fully charged, as Conni can tell from a quick look at the screen.

»Well, if this isn't an emergency, then I don't know what is!« she says, grabbing the mobile and wallet.

She takes her bike helmet from the cloaks cupboard, puts it on as she runs, and clicks the fastener under her chin.

---

to dial – wählen
engaged – *hier*: besetzt
to be jinxed – verhext sein

Seconds later, she is speeding on her mountain bike down the quiet residential streets. She turns into Ahornweg before crossing Fürst-Pückler-Allee at breakneck speed.
She doesn't slow down until she is at the bus station. The little headquarters building looks deserted. No sign of Mandy.
Conni **tears** the helmet off her head, chains her bike to a street-lamp and races up the couple of steps to the ›City Transport Authority Offices‹, as she reads on a white sign as she runs past.
She stops in a little **ante-room**. What now? She looks around in confusion.
A young man is coming out of a room, carrying two folders.
Conni **plucks up her courage**. »Excuse me. Could you tell me where the fare-dodging department is, please?«
The young man looks her up and down. Conni can feel herself going red.
»If you're wanting to pay a **Post-journey Travel Penalty**,« says the young man, »you can go straight to the cash office.«
A post-journey travel penalty?? Help! What is that supposed to mean?
Conni clears her throat. »No, no,« she says quickly. »I just want to pick someone up.«

---

to tear – reißen
ante-room – Vorraum
to pluck up one's courage – sich ein Herz fassen
post-journey travel penalty – nachträgliches Beförderungsentgelt

»Try Admin, room 22,« the young man says curtly. Without another word, he turns and disappears behind one of the doors.
»Thanks,« Conni murmurs.
On Room 22 is a sign saying: »Please knock and wait!« Conni knocks and waits. Nothing happens.
She knocks again, more firmly this time.
»Yes?« comes a muffled voice.
Conni cautiously opens the door and peers into the room. Sitting at a desk, half hidden by a computer monitor and a house-plant, is a red-headed woman. She **scrutinises** Conni over the edge of her spectacles.
»Sorry, I wanted –,« Conni begins politely. She gets no further.
»Conni!« comes a loud shout. *»Is that you?«*
»Mandy?!«
With one bound, Conni is in the room.
Mandy is sitting on a wooden chair by the window. When she sees Conni, she jumps up so suddenly that the chair tips over.
»Conni!« sobs Mandy. She flings her arms round Conni.
»Mandy,« Conni stammers. »Now, just calm down.«
Conni finds a **tissue** in the pocket of her denim jacket. It is rather battered, but at least clean and unused. She hands it to Mandy. »Blow your nose. You look a real fright!«

---

to scrutinise – eingehend prüfen, mustern
with one bound – mit einem Satz
tissue – Taschentuch

»I know.« Mandy blows her nose noisily into the tissue, but Conni is relieved to notice that she does at least manage something resembling a little smile.
»Can I help you?« asks the lady behind the **potted plant**.
Conni whirls round. »Erm, yes, I hope so,« she stammers. »Um, it's this …« Oh, keep your cool! she says crossly to herself. »My name is Conni Klawitter,« she says. Her heart is beating like mad. »Mandy is my exchange partner. She's from England and she was caught fare-dodging. I'd like to collect her.«
Her voice is trembling slightly. No wonder, thinks Conni. With all that stress!
»Hmm, that's right.« The lady picks up a piece of paper and scrutinises it. »Your friend's been reported. The penalty fare is forty euros.« She looks up.
»Forty euros?« Conni opens her eyes wide.
Mandy's lip trembles dangerously.
»Forty euros,« the lady repeats. »I've already explained it to your friend, but I don't think she understood me properly.«
»But I've not got forty euros!« I don't believe it! thinks Conni, adding in despair: »And anyway, Mandy wasn't **deliberately** fare-dodging! She thought her student ID card was also a bus pass. Maybe it's like that in England?«
»Well, that's a real shame,« says the clerk. »But rules are rules, I'm afraid there's nothing I can do.« She gives Mandy a **sympathetic** look. »I'm sorry.«

---

potted plant – Topfpflanze
deliberately – absichtlich
sympathetic – mitleidig

Conni suddenly remembers the mobile. »I'm just going to make a phone call,« she says to Mandy. »I'll be back in a minute!«

»Don't leave me alone!« wails Mandy.

»I'll be back in a second,« Conni replies. *»I just want to call my mum, okay? She will help us.«*

Mandy nods. *»Okay. Please hurry.«*

Conni slips out of the room and into the corridor, where she dials the direct-dial number at the clinic with trembling fingers.

Mum answers almost immediately. »Klawitter.«

»Mum!« Conni cries agitatedly. »Quick, I need your help! I'm in the Transport Authority office. They say Mandy's been fare-dodging, and they're keeping her here. I came to collect her and pay the **fine**, but there's not enough money. And now –«

»Slow down,« Mum interrupts her. »Where are you? What's happened?«

Conni swallows. Then she repeats, slowly, what has happened.

»Mandy's being held there?« Mum repeats in disbelief.

Conni nods. »Yes! I really don't know what to do!«

»Don't do anything,« Mum replies. »Stay where you are! I'll be with you in a few minutes. Poor Mandy,« she adds. »They can't just arrest a **minor**, never mind a foreign girl who doesn't understand our language! See you soon, Conni.«

---

fine – Bußgeld
minor – Minderjährige/r

»See you soon – and thanks!« Conni ends the call and breathes a sigh of relief.
As quickly as she can, she races back to the office to be with Mandy and to wait for her mum.

When Mum arrives, Mandy and Conni are **perching** next to one another on two rickety chairs, holding hands.
Conni jumps up. »Mum!«
»Hello, Conni,« says Mum. To Conni's great relief, she **wears a kindly expression**. *»Hello, Mandy.«*
»Hello, Mrs Klawitter,« Mandy mumbles, **embarrassed**.
»It's not her fault!« Conni tells her mother insistently. »She thought her new student ID card was a free bus pass or something like that. At any rate –«
»We'll talk about it later, okay?« Mum says quietly. »I'll speak to this lady first.« Smiling, she turns to the clerk. »Hello, I'm Conni's mother, Annette Klawitter. I think there's been a misunderstanding.«
Barely a quarter of an hour later, Conni and Mandy are outside, beaming from ear to ear.
»Wow, Mum,« says Conni admiringly. »How on earth did you manage that?«
»The lady was very nice,« says Frau Klawitter, smiling. »I've **lodged an appeal against** the penalty charge, and I hope that's the end of it.« She puts one arm round Conni and the

---

to perch – hocken
to wear a kindly expression – einen freundlichen Gesichtsausdruck haben
to be embarrassed – sich schämen
to lodge appeal against – Widerspruch einlegen

other round Mandy. »It was really just an unfortunate mistake that Mandy thought her school ID was a bus pass.«
»Yes, I did,« murmurs Mandy. »How could I be so blöd?«
»I think we'd better buy you a set of ten bus tickets right away,« Conni suggests.
Mandy nods, then gives Mum a kiss on the cheek, saying: »Thank you so much, Frau Klawitter. I'm sehr dankbar, für was Sie haben getan für mich. Mit ohne Ihre Hilfe ich hätte das nie geschafft!«
»And me?« says Conni, grinning. »What about me? How about a reward?«
»Oh yes!« Mandy immediately nods. »What about some Streuseln?«
Mum has to turn it down. »Sorry,« she says sadly, »but I have to get back to the clinic as quickly as possible.« She pulls out her **purse** and gives Conni a bank note. »But that doesn't mean that you should go without cake or ice cream. Have a nice afternoon and get over the shock.«
»Thanks, that's really cool,« says Conni, pleased. »Oh, there's one more thing ...« She pulls the mobile out of her pocket. »I took that with me, and the emergency wallet too.« She tells Mum about her **failed attempts** to call the practice and Dad's office. »Here, I imagine you'll want it back.«
»It's a good thing you took it with you,« says Mum. »That old thing really has turned out to be very useful.« She thinks briefly, then pushes the mobile back into Conni's hands. »You know what? You can keep it. For emergencies,« she

---

purse – Geldbeutel
failed attempts – fehlgeschlagene Versuche

adds. »Though I hope there won't be another one for a while!«

Conni gives a **squeal of delight**. »Really? I can keep the mobile?«

»Yes,« says Mum. »But don't lose it.«

»Not on your life!« Conni promises to look after the mobile as if her life and the Aztecs' golden treasure were both at stake. »Thank you!« she beams.

»It's fine,« says Mum. »But you can get your mobile working right now, and call me a taxi. Otherwise we'll still be here tomorrow morning!«

Conni giggles. And then she makes her second important call of the day on her very first mobile.

Wow, oh wow, she thinks, as she **keys in the number** of the taxi firm. You could write an entire novel about this afternoon!

---

sqeal of delight – Freudenschrei
to key in a number – eine Nummer eingeben

The next morning, Mandy's fare-dodging experience is the number one topic of conversation in the classroom.

»I'll never go by bus again so long as we're in Deutschland,« Alisha immediately declares. »Nie mehr will ich fahren mit eine deutsche Bus!«

»Me neither,« agrees Mandy. »Obwohl ich habe jetzt ein ten-trip ticket für die Bus.« She proudly holds up her brand-new ›Zehnerkarte‹. »Bitte sehr: mein Zehnfahrausweisschein!«

»It's called a ›Zehnerkarte‹,« laughs Conni. »But you'll **get the hang of it**!«

Janette looks up from the fashion magazine that she is flicking through. »Some people never get the hang of it,« she **hisses** in Mandy's direction. »Particularly not *her*!«

Vicky **screws up her nose** in agreement and carries on brushing her long blonde mane.

»We've got double sport in a minute, thank goodness,« growls Billi. »That's just what we need **to de-stress**.«

»What is she talking about?« asks Mandy.

»She says that sport is good for us,« Anna translates.

---

to get the hang of something – etwas hinkriegen
to hiss – zischen
to screw up one's nose – die Nase rümpfen
to de-stress – Stress abbauen

»*I* hoffe, dass wir werden spielen football,« sighs Louise. »Ich kann nicht länger überleben without it. Ich werde sick, ganz sicher!«

»Louise ist süchtig für Fußball,« Mandy whispers to Conni. »Sie ist ein echter champion und kann nicht leben ohne Ball.«

»Oh, I see.« Conni can't help grinning slightly. »Herr Albers is lovely. If we ask him really nicely, I'm sure he'll let us do two lessons of football.«

»Ich mach das!« beams Louise. »Für football ich würde machen alles!«

»Okay, we'll ask him,« says Conni. »And then Paul can see for himself how well you can play football. Maybe then he'll pull himself together and be a bit nicer to you.«

Louise **shrugs**. »Ach, das ist no problem. *I'm used to that,*« she says. »Ich bin gewöhnt daran, dass boys Probleme haben mit Fußballmädchen. Das ist in England so auch.«

»**All the same**, it won't hurt to show the boys,« says Anna. She holds her hand out to the others, and they all give a high five.

On the way to the sports hall they bump into Phillip, Paul and Toby.

»Hey, girls!« Phillip calls cheerfully. *»How are you?«*

»We are fine, thank you,« replies Conni. »Hello, Paul,« she says over Phillip's shoulder. »How's it going?«

Paul nods. »Fine. Why shouldn't it be?«

---

to shrug – mit den Schultern zucken
all the same – trotzdem

»Because you're about to lose to a girls' team,« **trills** Anna. She gives him a friendly look through her glasses.
»Eh?« replies Paul.
»We're going to ask Herr Albers to let us play football during the sports lesson,« explains Billi.
»And it's going to be us girls against you boys!« Anna stops and puts her hands on her hips. »So we can put an end once and for all to this stupid idea that girls don't know anything about football and stuff.«
Conni, Dina, Billi, Alisha, Kate, Mandy and Louise form a row next to Anna and pull determined faces.
»Exactly!« says Conni.
»Exactly!« growls Mandy.
Louise gives Paul an amused glance, silently pointing at a little **embroidered badge** on her football shirt. It bears the logo »Girl Power Brighton«.
»It is die beste Team in our school,« Toby whispers to Paul. *»Just girls, you know!«*
»A girls' team is the best team in your school?« Paul laughs. »Oh crikey!«

Herr Albers agrees immediately. »Of course,« he says. »A ball game outdoors is probably the best thing to do with such a big group. But why does it have to be boys against girls?«
»For personal reasons,« murmurs Louise.
»Aus persönlichen Gründen,« Billi translates, grinning.

---

to trill – *hier*: flöten
embroidered badge – gesticktes Abzeichen

Conni is looking forward to the match. If Louise really is as good as they all say, the boys don't stand a chance.
Janette and Vicky **simultaneously** twist their pretty faces into a grimace when they hear that they are to play football.
»No sports for me,« Vicky immediately declares, tossing back her long hair.
»I don't think I can join in either. I've left my sports kit at home,« says Janette to Herr Albers, emphasising her lie with a practised flutter of her eyelashes. »Vicky and I had better stay in the changing rooms.«
The two girls look like twins: they are wearing tight pink jeans and pink tops with glittery stars. They have even painted their finger-nails pink.
Herr Albers grins. »**Linesmen** don't need sports kit.« He presses two flags into their hands. »The fresh air will do you good!«
Janette is about **to object**, but the sports teacher turns round and just leaves her standing there.
Conni, Anna, Billi and Dina giggle.
»They really suit you, those pretty little flags,« says Anna.
»Though the red clashes rather with your **nail-varnish**,« grins Billi. »Really trendy pink. It kind of reminds me of marzipan piglets.«
Janette snorts with anger. »Come on!« she hisses to Vicky, Ariane and Saskia. »It stinks in here!«

---

simultaneously – gleichzeitig
linesman – Linienrichter
to object – protestieren, Einspruch erheben
nail-varnish – Nagellack

Louise pretends to screw her index finger into the side of her head. *»She's a real nutter, isn't she?«*

»What's a ›nutter‹?« asks Anna.

»It's a ›Spinnerin‹,« Billi translates.

»Oh, yes, that's right,« Anna says firmly to Louise. *»She's the biggest nutter in town!«*

Laughing, they get changed and walk with the other girls onto the big field next to the sports hall.

The boys are already waiting for them, their expressions **grim**.

Paul and Mark are trying **particularly** hard to look severe.

When the girls come trotting up to them, they kneel down in the grass, pretending to re-tie the laces of their football boots.

»Girls and football go as well together as **chimps** and nuclear physics –« Conni hears as she runs past them, »namely not at all! Ha, ha, ha!«

Chimps and nuclear physics? Conni raises an eyebrow. Just you wait! We'll see about that!

Janette and Vicky are standing on the sidelines, waving their flags half-heartedly. Although it is cloudy, they are both wearing huge sunglasses.

Louise gives them a cheerful wave.

Then Herr Albers holds up a coin. »**Heads or tails**?« he asks.

---

grim – grimmig
particularly – besonders
chimps – Schimpansen
heads or tails – Kopf oder Zahl

»Heads,« says Louise. The girls have unanimously voted her captain.
»Tails,« growls Paul, the boys' captain.
Herr Albers tosses the coin in the air. As it falls to the grass, Conni holds her breath.
»Heads!« the sports teacher calls. »Girls to kick off!« He raises the whistle to his lips and blows.
Janette drops her flag in horror and puts her hands over her ears.
And then it does all kick off – at such breathtaking speed that Conni and the others struggle to follow what is happening.
Louise pounces on the ball, leaves Mark and Toby standing helplessly on the halfway line, dribbles round Paul, and races unchecked to the opposing goal like an angry little **bull**.
Phillip is in goal. He spreads out his arms, takes in first the ball then Louise's determined face, and dives into the corner. The ball **whizzes** just past his left ear and slams into the net.
For a moment, it is so silent on the pitch that Conni can hear a bumble-bee buzzing in the grass.
Then Phillip curses loudly. »Rats!« He kicks the goalpost.
Conni thrusts her arm in the air. »Yes!«
»Goal!« cries Billi. »Goal!«
»Goal!« yells Mandy and Alisha.

---

bull – Stier
to whiz – zischen

The girls hug one another and leap around with joy. Even Janette and Vicky hold their flags up in the wind and wave them happily.
Louise shouts like mad. Then she races diagonally across the pitch, kisses the hem of her football shirt, does a forward roll, and is heartily congratulated by her team-mates.
Herr Albers blows his whistle. Play continues.
At half time, the girls are leading with seven goals. Louise has scored five of them.
Paul and Mark are pulling their hair out in despair. Phillip trots off the pitch, his head lowered, and allows Tim **to be sent on as a substitute** for him. »Is that embarrassing or what?« he groans.
Conni grins triumphantly. This kind of football is great fun!
»At least we got a consolation goal,« Mark murmurs when Herr Albers finally blows the whistle at the end of the second half. »Otherwise it would have been even more embarrassing.«
The girls do a lap of honour round the pitch, celebrating their **victory**.
»Nine – one.« Paul pulls a pained expression. »To the girls! Oh man …«
Paul has only one wish: to get into the shower and never get out again. Or **to be swallowed up** for all eternity **by the turf**. The girls' landslide victory has to be the most embar-

---

to be sent as a substitute – *hier*: eingewechselt werden
victory – Sieg
to be swallowed by the turf – vom Erdboden verschluckt werden

rassing thing that has ever happened to him! Simply incredible!
»I told you so,« Toby argues. »Aber ihr wolltet mir ja nicht glauben, dass Louis is so good!«
Paul wipes the sweat from his forehead with a towel. »Well, she's good …«
»Good isn't the word for it,« says Phillip. He puts a water bottle to his lips and drinks in long **gulps**. »She's unbeatable!«
»Yes, she's the perfect little player,« Tim murmurs admiringly. »She's bound to end up in the national team.«
The other boys agree.
»We should go and congratulate them,« Phillip suggests. »They **deserve** it.«
Paul nods. »Yes, otherwise we'd be bad losers.«
They join the girls who are trotting slowly round, lap after lap, and offer them their hands.
»Well done,« murmurs Paul. He runs alongside Louise. »You were brilliant! *Congratulations!*«
»Oh, thank you,« Louise replies, beaming. »Wenn du kommst nach Brighton, du kannst bekommen eine second chance, okay?«
»You mean a **return match**?« Paul gives her a sidelong look and grins. »Cool! That's very fair of you.« He raises his hand. Louise high-fives him and gives him an encouraging wink.
»See you in Brighton,« she says. *»A return match is a great idea!«*

---

gulp – Schluck
to deserve somthing – etwas verdient haben
return match – Rückspiel

»You're on.« Paul nods, satisfied. A return match – isn't that what professional footballers always do?
Conni is pleased. Why did it have to take this long? she thinks. Paul and Louise are made for one another: both think about nothing but football. No doubt they'll only be appearing with balls under their arms for the next few days.

***

While Mandy is at her language course that afternoon, Conni tidies her room a bit. Or, to be precise, half of her room: she leaves the other half to Mandy.
»Amazing, the way all this stuff **accumulates**,« Conni murmurs as she clears half of the desk, shoving note-pads and **jottings** into a drawer. School text books and exercise books go into her rucksack, where they belong, or on the shelf.
When she has finished, she casts a glance at Mandy's chaotic half.
My goodness, thinks Conni, I thought I collected every possible bit of stuff, but Mandy really does break all records: printed paper napkins, brightly coloured ice cream umbrellas, advertising flyers, books of matches – it seems that she even wants to keep the receipt for her raspberry lipgloss as a **memento**!
Conni grins. Well, why not?
She puts a little cardboard box on the table. If Mandy wants, she can keep her treasures in there. Then they at least won't

---

to accumulate – sich ansammeln
jottings – Notizen
memento – Andenken

go flying around the room when the hoover is switched on. Conni fetches the hoover and gets stuck into her work. Soon, the room is **unrecognisable**.

That evening, Paul's parents have invited Conni, Mandy, Mum, Dad and Jakob to a »German-British evening«. Conni is very excited.

»Bestimmt es gibt fish and chips,« Mandy enthuses hopefully. »Das ist Louises und mein Lieblingsessen.«

»That's these fish fingers with vinegar, isn't it?« Jakob pulls a face. »No, you can eat that on your own!«

»There's bound to be something for you too,« says Conni. »After all, it's supposed to be a German-British evening. So there'll be some yummy sausages on the barbecue as well. And Mum's made a huge bowl of potato salad. We're taking that with us.«

»Phew,« says Jakob, relieved.

When it starts, he is holding the bowl of potato salad out in front of him as reverently as if it were the **Crown Jewels**. Dad has brought little paper flags for Jakob to decorate the salad. Now the British Union Jack is right in the middle of the salad next to the German flag. Around them are the brightly coloured flags of the other nations. In the Hausers' front garden are **torches** lighting the way to the back garden, where a trestle table is set up. Around it are folding chairs with colourful cushions.

---

unrecognisable – nicht wiederzuerkennen
Crown Jewels – Kronjuwelen
torch – Fackel

Paul's father is already at the barbecue. Conni's dad immediately goes to join him. Within minutes, the two men are talking shop about the best temperature for grilling meat. There are already a couple of **chops** on the barbecue. A tempting aroma wafts through the garden.

When Conni and Mandy go to say hello to Herr Hauser, he visibly recoils.

Mandy, it's true, has made a particularly big effort with her outfit: she is wearing massive black laced boots and baggy jeans which are at least three sizes too big and have a massive tear around her bottom. The hem of her lime green t-shirt is frayed and, to celebrate, she has hung lots of little safety pins to her earrings. Conni has no choice but to admire Mandy for her **pluck** and inventiveness.

»Don't you mind, dass die Leute dich immer so anstarren?« she asks Mandy as Dad and Herr Hauser turn back to the barbecue.

»What does ›anstarren‹ mean?« she replies.

Conni explains. Mandy laughs.

»No, ich mag es, anders zu sein,« she says. »Es ist fun, nicht so normal und langweilig zu sein wie alle andere.«

Conni looks down at herself. As always, she is wearing jeans, a t-shirt and trainers. Practical and comfortable. The only noticeable thing about her is her new neon **hair bobble** – and that is barely visible. She suddenly feels horribly normal and boring.

---

chop – Kotelett
pluck – Mut
hair bobble – Haargummi

As if she can read her mind, Mandy says: »If you want, wir können machen eine ganz neue Conni aus dir!« Her eyes sparkle with delight. »Neue Haaren, neue Klamotten, neuer Look! *A brand-new Conni!* What denkst du?«

»Hmm, I'm not sure,« Conni says **hesitantly**.

Mandy grins. »Wenn du brauchst eine andere Look, frag mich. Ich kann dir geben viele Tipps. Ich bin eine, wie sagt man das? Experte.«

»What do you think the neighbours would say if I suddenly started going around with safety pins in my ears and ripped jeans,« Conni giggles. »Not to mention my parents!«

»So what?« Mandy shrugs. »Es ist egal, was die Leuten sagen.«

Maybe to you, Conni thinks, amused.

»I'll think about it, okay?« she finally says. »It does **appeal**. But just for fun!«

»Okay,« replies Mandy. *»Just for fun!«*

Jakob is listening in with interest, when a **jelly baby** suddenly lands on his head. Baffled, he looks up and sees Marie, who is sitting above him in the tree house with a grin all over her face.

»Pssst!« she says, letting down a rope ladder. Without hesitating, Jakob clambers up and quickly pulls the ladder up after him.

»Well, those two are occupied for now,« laughs Mum. She thanks Paul's mother for the invitation.

---

hesitantly – zögernd
to appeal – *hier*: es ist reizvoll
jelly baby – Gummibärchen

»Louise wanted to make something typically British for us today,« Frau Hauser confides, putting the potato salad on the table along with all the other tasty treats. »Oh, here's Frau Sandulescu! I thought I'd just invite her, given that we're all having a get-together.«

»How nice,« says Mum. »A real neighbourhood party!«

Frau Scandulescu, too, gives Mandy a curious look, but she smiles as she does so. She is precariously holding a **bulbous glass container** out in front of her. A red liquid is **sloshing** around inside it, and she carefully puts it in the middle of the table.

When she sees Conni's surprised look, she quickly says: »No, no, Conni! It's not what you think. Just some harmless punch made of red-coloured fruits!«

She winks conspiratorially and shakes Mandy's hand. »I like your hair,« she whispers to her. »The red goes perfectly with my fruit punch!«

Conni laughs. She remembers her neighbour once giving her the recipe for a **love-potion**. The **vital** thing was that it had to be bright red if it were to work – just as red as the liquid in Frau Sandulescu's glass container, and as red as Mandy's spiky hair!

Conni winks back, then feels someone pulling her t-shirt from behind.

---

bulbous glass container – bauchiges Glasgefäß
to slosh – schwappen
love-potion – Liebestrank
vital – entscheidend, wichtig

»Hi Conni! Ich habe versprochen zu machen fish and chips,« says Louise. »Will you and Mandy helfen mich in die Küche?«
»Of course I will!« Conni replies immediately.
»Me too,« Mandy nods.
Only Paul looks grumpy. »Oh no. Do I have to?«
»Yes!« chorus the girls.
Louise drags him along by the arm of his sweatshirt. »Du kannst falten die paper.«
»You want me to fold paper?« Paul frowns. »I don't have to wear a paper hat, do I?«
»Of course not,« Louise replies firmly. »Du sollst only Tüten falten.«
»Tüten – bags? Oh, yeah, right,« Paul murmurs. »Hopefully not **sick-bags**.« He gives a cheeky grin. »I mean, just in case we don't like the food.«
Louise rolls her eyes. »Oh please … Paulie,« she groans. »Tu nur was ich sage, and everything will be fine, okay?«
Paul retreats. »Okay, okay,« he says, still grinning. »I'll do anything you say!«
Conni and Mandy exchange amused looks. It is pretty clear who is wearing the trousers.

A couple of minutes later, Mandy and Louise are filling Paul's paper bags with roughly chopped **slivers** of potato and baked fish.

---

sick-bag – Spucktüte
sliver – Scheibe, Stück

And that's supposed to be tasty? Conni wonders to herself. The **grease** is already seeping through the thin paper! And then the **vinegar** – ugh!
»We have to serve it quickly!« cries Mandy. »Man muss es schnell servieren!« She presses bags into Conni's and Paul's hands and hustles them out of the kitchen. *»Hurry up! Quick, quick!«*
»There's no way I'm eating that,« Paul whispers to Conni, leaving a trail of vinegar behind him. »It's **revolting**!«
»We ought at least to try it,« Conni whispers back. »They've gone to so much trouble.«
»Oh well: Enjoy!« Paul says cheekily. He is about to make for the potato salad and chops when Louise holds a particularly large portion of fish and chips in front of his nose. *»This is for you, Paulie,«* she says, beaming at him. »Fußballer müssen gut essen, you know!«
»Oh, erm … *thank you,*« Paul stammers. He swallows and turns round, looking for help. But Conni just giggles and rolls her eyes.
»Looks as if we've got no choice,« she says, as Mandy also presses a portion of fish and chips into her hands.
Frau Sandulescu, too, is given a full paper bag.
»How marvellous,« she sighs. »I've not had fish and chips since forever! Or, to put it more precisely, since the last time I was in London – and that was many years ago.« She sniffs the air **expectantly**.

---

grease – Fett
vinegar – Essig
revolting – eklig
expectantly – erwartungsvoll

»Jakob! Marie!« calls Frau Hauser. »Aren't you hungry?«
»We'd rather eat jelly babies!« comes the reply. »And potato salad with sausages!«
Jakob's and Marie's faces appear at the door of the tree house.
»We'll let the basket down,« calls Marie. »You can put something in it for us.«
»But no fish in paper!« bellows Jakob.
There is a rustling in the leaves. Shortly afterwards, a little basket is let down on a rope.
Paul and Conni fill it with two bottles of juice, two portions of salad, a couple of barbecued sausages and some bread, and **tug** on the rope. The picnic basket makes its **wobbly** way back up through the branches.
»Cool!« comes from up above. »Thanks!«
»You're welcome!« Conni and Paul call back, then bravely set about their meal.
»I think it's an **acquired** taste,« Paul's father murmurs, discreetly disposing of his half-full bag behind the bread-bin.
»Indeed, indeed,« says Conni's father, chewing bravely.
Only Frau Sandulescu, Louise and Mandy polish off their portions with real enthusiasm, even returning to the kitchen for second helpings.

---

to tug – zupfen, ziehen
wobbly – wackelig
acquired – angeeignet, angewöhnt

Full, happy, and safe in the knowledge that fish and chips will probably never be among her favourite meals, a tired Conni slides into bed two hours later.

Mandy is running water in the bathroom, singing her favourite song.

»Das war eine very gemutliche Abend, wasn't it?« she says, as she is finally lying in bed, yawning.

»Yes, it really was ›gemütlich‹,« replies Conni. »And thanks to you and Louise for cooking for us!«

»Oh, es war eine Vergnügen,« Mandy says **airily**. »Tomorrow ich will machen apple crumble für alle!«

The two girls giggle and whisper for a short while longer. Then Conni turns out the light. The full moon **casts** its pale light into the room. The house is silent. Mau is lying in his basket next to Conni's bed, purring in his sleep as if he were dreaming. It really was ›gemütlich‹.

»Good night,« whispers Conni.

»Good night,« Mandy murmurs sleepily, **burping** quietly. *»Sweet dreams!«*

***

---

airily – leichthin
to cast – *hier*: werfen
to burp – rülpsen

When Conni hears a slight noise in the middle of the night, she thinks at first that she's been dreaming. But then she sees a shadow flitting across the room.
Mandy? she thinks sleepily, looking at the clock radio next to her bed. Half past one!
In the pale half-light of the moon, she can see Mandy **creeping** across the room on tiptoe and pulling the door shut behind her.
It doesn't look like sleepwalking, thinks Conni. All the same, she sits up and crawls out of bed to see what Mandy is up to. Maybe she feels ill and has gone **to be sick**? It wouldn't surprise her after those two giant portions of fish! Or is Mandy a sleepwalker after all? If so, she'll have to catch her and take her back to bed as quickly as possible!
Conni bangs her **shin** against the edge of the bed and **yelps** quietly. Then she opens the door a crack and peeps out onto the landing. Her parents' bedroom door is shut. There is no light coming from under the bathroom door. Either Mandy has gone to the loo in the dark, or she isn't in the bathroom at all. Conni frowns. So where is she then?
Suddenly she sees pale light coming from downstairs.
Conni shuffles to the top of the stairs and looks over the **banisters**. There is a pale blue-ish light coming from the living room. Is Mandy watching TV in secret?

---

to creep – *hier*: schleichen
to be sick – *hier*: sich übergeben
shin – Schienbein
to yelp – aufjaulen
banisters – Geländer

Cautiously, she makes her way down the stairs one step at a time, avoiding the ones that she knows will squeak.

Only when she is at the bottom does she dare to breathe again.

Mau has followed her, and is purring around her bare legs. Conni strokes his fur briefly and puts a finger to her lips.

»Shh! Be quiet, you hear me?«

At the living room door, she stops and opens her eyes wide. Mandy is sitting in her nightie at Mum's work station, tapping away at the keyboard with quick fingers.

»Mandy!« Conni cries. She has read that you shouldn't under any circumstances wake or surprise sleepwalkers, but something very different is obviously going on here.

»Conni!« Mandy whirls round and stares at Conni. *»What are you doing here?«*

»I was just about to ask you the same thing,« hisses Conni. »You can't go on Mum's computer in the middle of the night!«

Mandy knots her fingers in front of her chest.

»I … I couldn't sleep,« she whispers. »I only wollte sehen, ob E-Mails für mich sind angekommen von meine Brüder.«

»E-Mails?« Conni repeats. »Now?!«

Mandy suddenly puts her hands up to her face and starts sobbing. Conni can barely **make out** what she is trying to say.

»Ich haben solches Heimweh nach mein dog Harry,« Mandy **weeps**. »Ich wollte nur sehen, ob es ihm gut geht. *I'm sorry.*«

---

to make out – *hier*: verstehen
to weep – weinen

»You're homesick?« Conni comes a couple of steps closer. Mandy raises her head and nods. »*Yes, I do miss home.* But noch mehr als das, ich vermisse my dog!«
Conni raises her eyebrows. Oh wow! Mandy is homesick for her dog!
»But … but –« she begins. Curses! What are you supposed to say in this situation? She puts a kindly arm around Mandy's shoulders. »Don't you like it here with us?«
»Ja, very much sogar!« sniffs Mandy. »Das ist nicht die Problem.«
»So what is the problem?« asks Conni. »Why are you so homesick that you can't sleep at night?« As she imagines how she'd feel in Mandy's place, she starts to feel very sorry for her: completely alone in a strange country with a strange family. And then that **dreadful** experience with that stupid ticket inspector …
»Meine Brüder geben Acht auf Harry,« says Mandy. »I know dass sie gut auf ihn aufpassen. Trotzdem ich vermiss ihn schrecklich. My brothers versprechen mich zu senden eine Foto von Harry, so dass ich kann sehen, dass es ihm gutgeht. Ich nur wollte sehen, ob sie haben die Foto geschickt.«
Conni's **expression** slowly **clears**. She rubs her hands and grins. »Move up a bit,« she says. »Then we can see if you've had any mail!«
Before Mandy can say anything, Conni has pulled the keyboard over and has logged in. »Anyway, you'd never have got

---

dreadful – schrecklich, furchtbar
expression clears – Miene hellt sich auf

in without me,« she giggles. »Mum keeps her password dead secret!«

A couple of clicks later, she is in Mandy's inbox, and Mandy is sorting through her new mail.

»There it is!« she cries excitedly, opening an attachment.

On the screen appears a picture of a big black dog. His **amber** eyes smile at Mandy and Conni.

»Well and happy,« says Conni. »I don't think you need to worry about him in the slightest. He looks absolutely gorgeous, really sweet.«

»That's my Harry …« sighs Mandy.

Conni turns the **printer** on and prints the picture out in colour.

»Here you go,« she says, passing it to Mandy. »So you can sleep better.«

»Thank you so much, Conni,« Mandy whispers. *»You are a very good friend!«*

Mandy quickly types an email to her brothers, then Conni switches the computer off.

»Time to go to sleep,« she yawns.

»I guess so,« replies Mandy, pressing the picture of the dog to her chest.

It is just as well that Mum and Dad **sleep** so **soundly**, thinks Conni, once she is lying in bed again, Mau purring contentedly beside her.

***

---

amber – bernsteinfarben
printer – Drucker
to sleep soundly – tief schlafen

At school, neither of them mentions Mandy's homesickness and their **nocturnal** computer session. They have decided that it should remain their secret.

»*Good friends sometimes have secrets,*« Mandy has said.

And Conni has agreed.

That morning, the exchange students are supposed to be talking about themselves and their school. Mandy has brought the photo of Harry. When it is her turn, she passes it around the class. She tells them that Harry is a trained **rescue dog** who is used on the beach in Brighton during the summer months to save bathers from **drowning**.

»Oh, he's so cute,« says Anna. »What a shame you can't bring him with you!«

»Ja, very schade.« Mandy nods, smiling. »Aber es geht ihm gut. *I know he's fine.*« She winks almost **imperceptibly** at Conni. Conni gives her a thumbs-up and grins.

Louise talks about her football team and lists the numerous tournaments and cups that she's won. Paul and the other boys turn ever more **pale** as they listen.

»This afternoon there's no language course for our guests,« says Frau Lindmann just before the end of school. »Tomorrow morning we're going to the natural history museum in Burgstadt. We're meeting in the school car park at quarter to eight.« She looks at Conni, Mandy and Louise. »Make sure

---

nocturnal – nächtlich
rescue dog – Rettungshund
drowning – Ertrinken
imperceptibly – unmerklich
pale – blass

you arrive on time. The bus is leaving at eight. Anyone who's late will have to spend the morning with the parallel class.« Conni decides to set her alarm for ten minutes earlier. She knows that the Dragon isn't quick to let up once she's got her eye on you. Being late again is quite out of the question!

»Was haltet ihr davon, einen apple crumble zu backen heute Nachmittag?« Mandy asks on the way to the bike-stands.
Conni immediately agrees. »I'm sure Mum won't mind. We'll just have to go shopping,« she says.
Louise shakes her head **regretfully**. »I promised den boys, mit ihnen football zu spielen. I'm sorry.«
Anna and Alisha **decline**, too.
»We're going riding today,« Anna explains. »My riding teacher said that Alisha could join in with a riding lesson.«
»How lovely for you,« says Conni, »and what a shame for us.« She turns to Billi, Dina and Kate. »You've presumably already made plans too?«
»No,« grins Billi. »**At any rate**, none that I know of.«
Kate and Dina laugh.
»Count me in,« says Dina.
»Me too,« adds Kate.
»Brilliant!« Conni counts. »That makes five of us.«
»Exactly right, you mathematical genius,« says Billi. »And your mum presumably won't mind us using your kitchen?«

---

regretfully – bedauernd
to decline – *hier*: ablehnen
at any rate – jedenfalls

»No, I'm sure she won't.« Conni is quite certain. She reaches into her rucksack and grins. »All the same, I'd rather ask her first. Why else have I got a mobile?«
A quick phone call confirms what Conni has thought: her mum has no **objections**. Campaign Apple Crumble can begin!
»We'd better get everything that we need on the way home,« she says to Mandy. »I'm sure I've got enough money. Do you know the **ingredients** off **by heart**?«
Mandy nods. Conni looks in her purse while the others say goodbye.
»We'll be at yours at around three, okay?« says Billi.
»Three's perfect,« replies Conni.
Anna and Alisha are already wheeling their bikes out of the school playground.
»Save us a piece!« Anna calls over her shoulder.
»Will do!« Conni calls back. »If there's any left!«

Outside the shopping centre, Conni and Mandy lock their bikes together and put their helmets under their arms.
»What do we need for your ***recipe****?«* asks Conni. She is starting to find it quite natural to ask Mandy in English for the baking ingredients.
»Oh, it's pretty simple,« replies Mandy. »Wir brauchen Äpfeln of course, butter, sugar, flour, cinnamon and a lemon.«

---

objections – Einwände
ingredients – Zutaten
by heart – auswendig
recipe – Rezept

»Okay.« Conni screws up her nose. »Äpfel, Butter, Zucker, Mehl, eine Zitrone … fine. But what's ›cinnamon‹?«

»Ich weiß nicht the German word for it.« Mandy shrugs. *»I'm sorry.«*

»Hmm,« says Conni. »I fear we might have a little problem.« She looks round, **pondering**. »But I think we can solve it. The supermarket is on the ground floor.«

»I see.« Mandy nods. »Aber was hat das zu tun mit unsere Problem?«

»Easy!« laughs Conni. »First we'll go to the second floor, to the bookshop. There we'll grab a dictionary and have a look at what ›cinnamon‹ is!«

»Great idea!« says Mandy, giving Conni a high five. *»Let's go!«*

As they take the **escalator** to the second floor, they pass a chemist's shop.

»Look!« exclaims Mandy. »Sie haben dieselbe raspberry lip gloss, das ich habe gekauft ein paar Tage vorher!«

»Of course it sells lip gloss,« says Conni. »Why, have you finished yours already?«

»No, aber ich möchte noch eine davon kaufen. Als Souvenir, you know?« Mandy cranes her neck to see, and almost stumbles over the last step of the escalator.

»Let's look first and see what ›cinnamon‹ is in German,« says Conni, »and on the way back, you can buy as much lip gloss as you like, okay?«

---

to ponder – überlegen
escalator – Rolltreppe

The bookshop is small and clearly arranged. Conni has no trouble finding an English-German dictionary on the shelves. She opens it at C, and flicks through a few pages.
»Oh, I see!« She smiles. »Here is it: cinnamon … oh, I should have thought of it myself!«
»Was ist es in German?« Mandy asks curiously.
»›Zimt‹,« says Conni, putting the book back. »Plain, **straightforward** ›Zimt‹!«
»All right, dann wir fahren jetzt in die Erdgeschoss und kaufen die Zimt,« says Mandy. »Aber before that, ich kaufe mein lip gloss, okay?«
A couple of minutes later, Mandy is standing at the **till** with a little tub of her favourite raspberry lip gloss.
»Satisfied now?« grins Conni.
»Very ›zufrieden‹!« Mandy puts the little tub into her rucksack and carelessly stuffs the **receipt** into her denim jacket. »*Now we can go and find the* ›Zimt‹!«

The supermarket is completely empty. **In a jiffy**, a kilo of apples, a packet of cinnamon, a lemon and all the other ingredients are in the shopping trolley. As Conni pays, she is already looking forward to baking. All the ingredients of apple crumble are ones that she likes. The end result looks set to be delicious.
They are about to leave the shopping centre with their full plastic bag when a man suddenly blocks their way.

---

straightforward – *hier*: einfach
till – Kasse
receipt – Kassenzettel
in a jiffy – gleich, sofort

»**Bag search**,« he says, holding up his ID for a fraction of a second. »This way, please!«
Mandy jumps in horror.
Conni stands still and looks the man up and down. He looks very young, and is wearing jeans and trainers.
»May I see your ID again?« she asks politely.
»You come along with me first,« growls the man. He makes a lunge for Conni's elbow, but she vigorously shakes his hand off. »No way!« she snaps at him. Her voice trembles with **indignation**. She has no idea where she's summoned up the courage. It is suddenly there. »You show me your ID first! You could be anyone!«
Two old women stop and shake their heads.
»They've caught a couple more,« one of them mutters. »In broad daylight, too. They just get more and more **brazen**.«
The other points to Mandy. »Look at her! You can see what's wrong with her just by looking.«
Conni gives the women a fierce look. They turn and quickly go on their way.
»What's up?« asks Mandy. »Was möchte diese Mann?«
»No idea,« says Conni. »That's what I'd love to know.«
The young man sighs and holds his ID under Conni's nose.
»*Now* are you going to come with me?« he asks irritably.
»Securus Ltd., Ulrich Fuchs, Store Detective,« Conni reads under her breath. A cold chill suddenly runs down her

---

bag search – Taschenkontrolle
indignation – Empörung
brazen – dreist

spine. A store detective? What's that all about? They've not done anything!
»Okay, we're coming,« she says, clutching her shopping bag. Has she perhaps forgotten to pay for something?
She quietly tries to think about what is in the bag. There is a rushing noise in her ears, and her brain is muddling everything up. No! She shakes her head **vigorously**. No way!
»It has to be a mistake,« she murmurs.
»We'll soon see about that,« says the detective. »Into my office, please.«
»What's he talking about?« Mandy asks quietly *»What does he want?«*
»I have no idea,« Conni replies truthfully. »I don't know.«
Their knees **trembling**, the two girls walk along in front of the store detective. They have to make their way right across the shop. Conni feels as if everyone is staring at her. She's never felt so awful in her entire life.
When they are finally sitting in a stuffy little office that stinks of stale cigarette smoke, the detective takes their shopping bag and puts it on the desk.
»The receipt's in there,« Conni says **hoarsely**. She clears her throat. »I paid 9 Euros 79. I know it for a fact.«
Mandy is sitting next to her, her head bowed. Conni takes her hand, squeezes it, and sighs. Her need for exciting experiences has long since been satisfied!

---

spine – *hier*: Rücken
vigorously – energisch
to tremble – zittern
hoarsely – heiser

When the shopping is lined up on the table, the store detective compares it to the receipt.
»Okay,« he says. »Now empty your pockets please.«
»Why?« Conni's courage turns into anger. »We've not stolen anything!« Her eyes flash at Herr Fuchs. »Are you actually allowed to do this?«
»No,« he admits. »We can wait for the police instead.«Police? Conni thinks. Oh help, not the police!She turns her pockets inside out. Apart from an opened packet of chewing gum and an old cinema ticket, there is nothing in there.
Mandy copies her, putting the contents of her pocket on the table.
»Maybe he thinks we're terrorists?« she whispers to Conni.
»That's how he's treating us, at any rate,« growls Conni.
Herr Fuchs examines the contents of Mandy's pockets: the crumpled receipt from the make-up department, her tub of lip gloss from the little shop in town, the ›Zehnerkarte‹ for the bus, a used tissue …
Frowning, he **flattens out** the till receipt. »Open your rucksacks, please.«
Conni rolls her eyes. That on top of everything else! She **undoes** her school bag and presents the detective with her school books. He just casts a brief glance inside, and nods.
When Mandy opens her rucksack, he examines the contents rather more **closely**. He finally reaches inside, pulls the new lip gloss out, and puts it next to the other one on the table.

---

to flatten out – *hier*: glattstreichen
to undo – aufmachen
closely – *hier*: genau

»Two lots of lip gloss,« he says, »but just one receipt.« He scrutinises Mandy. »Can you explain that to me?«
Mandy stares at him. *»What do you mean? I don't understand a word you are saying!«*
»Is your friend a foreigner?« he asks, turning to Conni.
Conni nods. »Mandy's an exchange student from Great Britain, and I want to ring my parents this instant.« She takes a deep breath. »I don't think you can just keep us here like this!«
Herr Fuchs rubs his chin with one hand. With the other hand, he points to the little tub of lip gloss. »Your friend has two lots of lip gloss, but has evidently only paid for one,« he says. »She's under suspicion for **shoplifting**. That being the case, I have the right to keep you here until the police come and make their report.« He reaches for the telephone.
Conni jumps up. »Police? Hang on a minute! My friend only bought one of the lip glosses here. The other one came from the chemist's in the **pedestrian precinct**!«
»Then your friend is **bound to** have the receipt for it, isn't she?« Herr Fuchs leans forward. »You show me the receipt, and everything will be fine. Until then I will unfortunately have to assume that one of the tubs was stolen from here.«
»For God's sake!« Conni drops back down onto the chair. »You can see that Mandy's already used one of them!«
»That's no **proof** of anything,« retorts Herr Fuchs.

---

shoplifting – Ladendiebstahl
pedestrian precinct – Fußgänderzone
to be bound to – *hier*: müssen
proof – Beweis

Wide-eyed, Mandy has been following their exchange. Conni bites her lower lip, thinking madly.
»Receipt, receipt …,« she murmurs, »now, there was something …« She stares at the wall. »Got it!« she suddenly cries. »The till receipt for the first lip gloss is on my desk! I put it there myself!«
»How nice,« says Herr Fuchs. »What a shame it's no use to either of us there.«
»I'll go and get it! I'll only be a few minutes on my bike!« Conni is already reaching for her helmet.
Mandy clings on to her sleeve, horrified. *»You can't leave me alone like this!«*
Conni hesitates. No, she really can't leave Mandy here on her own. Rats … grinding her teeth, she puts the helmet down.
»Is there anyone in your family who could bring us the till receipt?« Herr Fuchs asks in the **tense** silence.
Conni looks at him briefly. I should ring Dad, she thinks. But he'd make a terrible fuss and come straight here before going to fetch the stupid till receipt. That would all take far too long. And anyway he's probably in a meeting at the moment and –
No! She shakes her head. Dad wouldn't be much help at this particular moment. That just leaves Mum, but she isn't at home. And it would of course be Thursday that she had her long day at the practice. Just a minute! Conni's face brightens. Yes, that is it! Jakob always eats at the Hausers' on Thursday lunchtimes. And they have a house key for emergencies!

---

tense – angespannt

»I'll ring Paul!« she says excitedly to Mandy. »A friend,« she explains to Herr Fuchs. »He'll help us! No doubt about it!« she adds.

»**Be my guest**,« sighs the detective.

Conni quickly **dials** Paul's number. »Keep your fingers crossed,« she says to Mandy.

»Hello, Frau Hauser, it's me, Conni. Is Paul there?« It takes a minute for Paul to come to the phone. Conni chews her finger nails anxiously.

»Paul!« she cries when he finally answers. »You have to help us! Mandy and I are in trouble!« Paul is about to say something, but Conni interrupts him. »I'll tell you everything later when there's time, okay? No, there really isn't time now. Listen: you take our house key and go into my room. On my desk, there's a **pile** of receipts. Right at the top is a receipt from the chemist's in the pedestrian precinct. Yes, you heard right. You get that one, then come as quickly as you can to the shopping centre by the park, okay?«

Conni is **clutching** the mobile and nodding. »Yes, exactly. We're here in the shopping centre office, waiting for you. No, Paul, it's not some stupid joke. Honestly – I swear!« Frowning, she listens and nods again. »Yes, fine. See you soon, and –,« Conni swallows, »hurry up, okay?« She presses the ›end call‹ button and puts the mobile down. »He said he'd be here in ten minutes.«

---

be my guest – *etwa*: bitte sehr
to dial – wählen
pile – Stapel, Haufen
to clutch something – sich an etwas klammern

»Then we can deal with the formalities **in the meantime**.« Herr Fuchs pulls out a biro and waves an ash-grey form at them. »Have you got your IDs?«

»What for?« asks Conni.

»So I can **record your details**,« says Herr Fuchs.

Conni shakes her head. »I think you can save yourself the effort. This is all going to be sorted out in a few minutes anyway.«

The detective puts down the biro. »You're pretty **stubborn**. Has anyone ever told you that?«

»No,« says Conni. »But I can't stand being unfairly treated.«

»Would you like a drink?« Herr Fuchs asks in a slightly more friendly tone. »Coke, lemonade or juice?«

Conni and Mandy exchange **glances**.

»Juice, please,« growls Mandy.

Conni nods. »I'll have juice too.«

Herr Fuchs stands up and goes out into the corridor.

Conni hears some coins clinking, and then the noise of a drinks machine.

»Paul should be here any minute now,« she whispers softly to Mandy. »Don't worry.«

Mandy just nods. She is very pale.

Holding two cartons of juice, Herr Fuchs comes back in. Conni and Mandy thank him.

---

in the meantime – in der Zwischenzeit
to record someone's details – Personalien aufnehmen
stubborn – *hier*: hartnäckig
glance – Blick

As they are drinking, Conni wonders who really is shoplifting at that moment. Herr Fuchs doesn't seem to be worrying about that. He sits at his desk as **cool as a cucumber**, doodling on his blotter. He probably has a couple of colleagues, Conni thinks. In a shopping centre like this, there is presumably heaps of stuff stolen. She jumps when a knock comes at the door.

»Come in!« calls Herr Fuchs.

Please let it be Paul! thinks Conni. She clutches her carton of juice tightly.

Louise cautiously **pokes her head into** the little office. Next to her, Paul's head appears.

»Louise?« Mandy says, astonished.

»Paul!« cries Conni. She jumps up, pulls the door open, and flings her arms round him. »Wow, I'm so pleased to see you!«

»Eh, erm, what?« Paul turns a bit red and frees himself from the violent embrace. »Erm, yes, here we are. Louise insisted on coming too.«

»Yes, great! So? Have you brought the receipt?« Conni asks wildly.

»'Course I have.« Paul holds up the little cardboard box from Conni's desk. »But there were so many bits of paper lying around that I thought I'd better bring all of them. But why do you need them? What's actually going on here?«

Conni grabs the box. »I'll tell you later, okay? First off, I need that stupid receipt!«

---

cool as a cucumber – seelenruhig

to poke one's head into something – den Kopf in etwas hineinstecken

She **rummages frantically through** Mandy's bits of paper.
»Ha!« she cries. »I knew it!« With a triumphant look, she holds up a **crumpled** till receipt. »One tub of raspberry lip gloss for 4 Euros 99. Bought on Tuesday in the chemist's in Fürsten-Passage!« She hands Herr Fuchs the receipt. »There you go! Do you believe us now?«
The store detective compares the receipt with the opened tub, then nods. »Yes, I think that's all in order.«
He stands up and holds his hand out to Conni. »I think I **owe you an apology**. I'm very sorry.«
Conni folds her arms across her chest. »I think you'd better apologise to Mandy,« she says. »After all, she's the one you accused.«
»Yes, you're right.« He scratches his chin and smiles, embarrassed. *»I am very sorry Mandy,«* he says in halting English, and shakes Mandy's hand. *»You can go home. Everything is okay.«*
His accent is terrible. Mandy raises her eyebrows. *»Well then,«* she murmurs, slipping her arm through Conni's. *»Let's go.«*
Quick as a flash, the girls pack their shopping back into the bag and leave the office, breathing a sigh of relief.
Herr Fuchs **accompanies** them to the door.
»Take care,« he says. »And, once again: I'm sorry!«

---

to rummage frantically through something – etwas angespannt durchwühlen
crumpled – verknittert
to owe someone an apology – jemandem eine Entschuldigung schuldig sein
to accompany someone – jemanden begleiten

»See you,« Conni says shortly. Never again! she thinks angrily.

Outside, her knees suddenly start trembling. »I think I need to sit down for a moment.«

Mandy sits down next to her on a little bench. *»That was horrible, wasn't it?«*

»You can say that again,« sighs Conni, taking a deep breath.

»Hey, you don't half seem to be having a ›Pechsträhne‹. First of all there was that fare-dodging business, and now this stuff here …«

»What's a ›Pechsträhne‹?« asks Mandy.

»A run of bad luck,« Louise translates.

Mandy laughs. »Oh yes! That's exactly was ich habe!«

»So are you finally going to tell us what was going on there?« Paul **interjects**.

»You saved our lives,« Conni says **drily**. »But now we're going home to make apple crumble. I'm in urgent need of something sweet. And anyway, we're meeting Billi, Dina and Kate. Are you coming?«

On the way to the bike stands, Conni **gives** Paul **a brief account of** what has happened.

»Unbelievable!« Paul shakes his head. »Just imagine if Mandy hadn't kept the receipt! Then you'd still be sitting in that detective's stuffy office!«

---

to interject – einwerfen

drily – trocken

to give someone a brief account of something – jemandem etwas knapp schildern

»I'd rather not imagine that,« Conni says soberly. She stops. »You know what? To celebrate our release, we'll invite you for apple cake!«
Paul and Louise look at one another, then both nod.
»We were going to play football,« says Paul, grinning, »but I never could say no to apple cake. Of course we'll come! I only had five pancakes for lunch. My stomach's in urgent need of a **refill**.«
»Cool!« Conni stuffs the bag into her bike basket.
»Then off we go!« she cries, setting off. »I've seen enough of that shopping centre to last me a hundred years!«

---

refill – *hier*: Nachschlag, Nachschub

»You can chop die Äpfel klein, Paulie,« says Mandy to Paul. She presses a vegetable knife into his hands. »Can you slice them thin, please?«

»Slice them thin?« Paul has a question mark written all over his face. The girls giggle.

»You need to cut the apples into ›schmale Spalten‹,« Conni explains. »But I'd **peel** them first if I were you.«

»Ah, right.« Using the knife, Paul gets to grips with the apple while Conni and Mandy make a **crumble topping** with butter, sugar, flour and a bit of cinnamon powder.

Louise, meanwhile, is greasing a baking dish.

»After that, du musst die Äpfeln tricklen mit die Zitrone,« she says casually. With her elbow, she **shoves** the lemon squeezer in Paul's direction.

Paul's **hair** almost **stands up on end**. »What on earth's ›tricklen‹?« he asks.

»›Träufeln‹,« says Conni. »You have to ›träufeln‹ – trickle, drizzle – lemon juice over the apple slices to stop them going brown.«

»Ah, I get it,« Paul grumbles. »No fear – I'm an expert apple-slicer and lemon-drizzler!«

---

to peel – schälen
crumble topping – Streusel
to shove – schieben
someone's hair stands on end – jemandem stehen die Haare zu Berge

Conni laughs.

When the doorbell rings, she goes to the door and opens it.

»Hi, you guys!« she greets Billi, Dina and Kate. »We've already started. I hope you don't mind.«

»No,« says Billi. »Or, at any rate, not unless you've already **gobbled everything up**.«

When she sees Paul, she raises her eyebrows. »What a strange **sight**: a man in the kitchen!«

»Ha, ha,« retorts Paul.

Louise takes the sliced apples from him and puts them in the **baking dish**. Mandy sprinkles the crumble topping over them and puts the baking dish into the oven.

»Thirty minutes,« she says. »Es braucht dreißig Minuten.«

»What temperature does the oven need to be?« asks Conni.

»Two hundred degrees,« says Mandy. »Bei zweihundert Graden ist alles perfekt.«

As the wonderful aroma of apples and cinnamon begins to fill the kitchen, Conni tells Dina and Billi about their terrible experience in the shopping centre.

Dina turns pale with horror.

»What an idiot!« Billi snaps, outraged. »How on earth could he think you were shoplifters? Well, I'm certainly not going in there again!«

---

to gobble everything up – alles verschlingen
sight – Anblick
baking dish – Backform

»No idea why he **pounced on** us of all people. Maybe he is bored, or maybe he thinks all girls of our age are suspicious. What do I know? Anyway, he did apologise to us,« Conni says. »But all the same … it was awful. I felt so helpless.« She shakes herself. »I won't be going back in there in a hurry!«

»Me neither,« says Mandy.

»You are pretty unlucky girls,« says Kate. »Wie sagt man in German? Pechmädchen?«

The others laugh. »No,« says Billi. »Pechvögel – unlucky birds!«

Ting-a-ling! goes the kitchen timer. Mandy stands up and inspects the apple crumble through the glass door of the oven. »Es braucht *five more minutes*,« she declares. »Wollen wir noch ein bisschen double cream dazu?«

»What please?« asks Paul.

»It's like whipped cream, but it's not sweet,« says Billi.»Then I vote for whipped cream!« says Paul.Conni gets out the hand-mixer, a tall **beaker** and the cream.

In no time at all, the whipped cream is ready.

»Perfect!« exclaims Louise. She turns the oven off and takes the baking dish out with the help of a pair of **oven gloves**. The crumble topping has turned into a crispy crust on top of the baked apples. Conni sniffs the air expectantly. It smells a bit like Christmas.

---

to pounce on someone – sich auf jemanden stürzen
beaker – Becher
oven glove – Ofenhandschuh, Topflappen

While Dina, Billi and Kate **lay the table**, Conni and Mandy wash up the baking things. And then it is apple crumble time!

»Mmm, is that tasty or what?« Billi says after taking her first bite. Conni shuts her eyes with pleasure. »Brilliant,« she murmurs. Dina nods enthusiastically. »You absolutely have to give me the recipe!« Paul is already helping himself to his second portion, which he covers with a mountain of whipped cream. »What?« he asks, grinning, when he sees the others' amused faces. »Boys need more calories than girls. It's scientifically proven!«

»Poor Paulie,« says Louise. »You'll have to do a lot of running, um wieder in good shape zu kommen.«

»I'm in very good shape already,« Paul retorts, unfazed. »I'll prove it on the football pitch tomorrow, *no worries*.«

»Maybe wir sollten drei Portionen übrig lassen für Jakob und Mr and Mrs Klawitter,« Mandy suggests. She puts three pieces onto a spare plate and covers them with foil. »Bestimmt sie werden es mögen.«

»Definitely!« says Conni. »Mum, Dad and Jakob all **have a** really **sweet tooth**!«

At that moment, Mau comes round the corner and **sidles** around the table, miaowing. Conni puts a bit of watered-down cream in his bowl. A short while later, they can hear

---

to lay the table – den Tisch decken
to have a sweet tooth – eine Naschkatze sein
to sidle – schleichen

only the sound of him **lapping** happily. It really is **cosy** in the little kitchen.
It's just a pity that Anna, Phillip and the other exchange students aren't here, Conni thinks. But maybe they can repeat Operation Apple Crumble once more before Mandy and the others have to go home.
Only four more days … Conni sighs. She doesn't want to imagine what it will be like, having to say goodbye to Mandy.
I'm bound to cry, she thinks. She swallows and quickly focuses on her apple crumble.
Mandy smiles across at her over the baking dish. Conni smiles back. What a shame that Brighton is such a long way away!

***

That evening, Mandy phones home and spends ages talking to her parents, her brothers and even to Harry the dog, who barks **as if on command** when he hears her voice.
Afterwards, Mum gives her permission to surf the internet for a bit and write some emails.
Conni has made herself comfortable in her bedroom, and is writing her diary. So much has happened today, she thinks. Where to start? Best to start with something positive, she decides. The crumble recipe, for example! By now, Conni knows it off by heart.

---

to lap – *hier*: auflecken
cosy – gemütlich, behaglich
as if on command – wie auf Befehl

MANDY LIVINGSTON'S APPLE CRUMBLE

500g apples
100g butter
100g sugar
175g flour
Cinnamon (Zimt!) to taste
1 lemon for drizzling

Peel and slice apples, then drizzle with lemon juice and put them in a baking dish (**pre-greased!**). Rub butter, sugar, flour and cinnamon together to make crumble topping, and spread on top of apples.

Bake for **approx.** 30 mins at 200°C and serve with whipped cream (Schlagsahne).

WARNING: HIGHLY ADDICTIVE!

Then she writes about her and Mandy's experience in the shopping centre. Everything, right from the start. She writes almost three pages, ending with:

> I don't know what would have happened if Paul hadn't helped us. It's great the way he just came and didn't ask stupid questions. I'll never forget it!

---

pre-greased – vorher eingefettet
approx. – *kurz für*: approximately – ungefähr

He's a brilliant friend!
Mum and Dad said the detective shouldn't have searched our bags. But then the police would have come. And that would have been even more embarrassing, wouldn't it?

Lost in thought, Conni puts down her pen. Mum and Dad had, of course, been horrified at supper when she'd told them the story of Herr Fuchs and his mean **suspicions** – but it had happened, and there was nothing they could do to change that fact.
»Why didn't you ring us?« Mum had asked. »Dad and I would have been straight over!«
Conni and Mandy had exchanged a long look, and then Mandy had said: *»We **managed** it with the help of our friends.«*
Precisely, thinks Conni. We managed it with the help of our friends!
She shuts the diary and puts it back into her bedside drawer.
Suddenly, she has an idea. She gets up and goes to her desk. Right at the bottom of one of the drawers is an old friendship book. Conni pulls it out, **scrambles** back into her cosy bed, and flicks through it.
She's had it since Year Four, and it is already pretty full.
The most recent entry is by Phillip:

---

suspicions – Verdächtigungen
to manage something – etwas schaffen
to scramble – *hier*: klettern

YYUR
YYUB
ICUR
YY4ME!

Next to it is a little photo of him grinning just as **impudently** as in real life.
Conni smiles at the rhyme. He presumably couldn't think of anything better than that. Typical Phillip!
She pulls the narrow bookmark out and chooses a new page. Perfect.
When Mandy comes quietly into the room, Conni sits up.
»Here,« she says. »Would you mind writing something in this?«
Mandy takes the book, which is covered in blue denim **fabric**, and strokes it. ›My Friends‹, it says in embroidered letters.
»My Friends,« says Mandy. *»That's so cool!«* She looks at Conni. »Ich will sehr gerne etwas schreiben darin. Soll ich gleich anfangen?«
»No, **take your time**.« Conni folds her arms behind her head and yawns. »You're still here for a couple more days,« she says. Fortunately, she adds silently.

YYUR, YYUB, ICUR, YY4ME! – geläufiger Spruch für Freundschaftsbücher, bedeutet: Too wise you are/Too wise you be/I see you are/Too wise for me! – Du bist zu klug/Du wirst immer zu klug sein/Ich sehe es ein/Du bist zu klug für mich
impudently – frech
fabric – Stoff
take your time – lass dir Zeit

Mandy nods. *»My friends,«* she murmurs once again.
Quick as a flash, she brushes her teeth, slips into her **nightie**, and snuggles down in her bed by the window.
Conni's eyes have already shut. Her breathing is quiet and regular, and she is smiling slightly.
»Good night,« Mandy whispers to her. *»See you in the morning.«*

---

nightie – Nachthemd

»Don't touch anything!« Conni hisses to Mandy as they enter the natural history museum in Burgstadt the next morning. »There are alarms and **security guards** all over the place. I really don't want to end up in some stuffy office, **being interrogated** again.«

Mandy giggles softly. *»Hey, calm down,«* she says. *»I won't touch a thing.* Ich werde sein ein very good girl der ganze Tag.«

»That's all right then,« says Conni.

The class is standing in the museum **entrance lobby** between a giant stuffed turtle, a dinosaur skeleton and several big glass cases.

Conni had once been to this museum in the nearby town when she was at primary school, but that was yonks ago. She looks around interestedly. The glass cases are filled with fossils, ancient pieces of jewellery and hand-crafted **tools** and weapons.

Billi really is in her element. She walks round the dinosaur skeleton in awe, whispering: »Wow! Have you ever seen anything like this?«

---

security guards – Wachleute
to be interrogated – verhört werden
entrance lobby – Eingangsbereich
tool – Werkzeug

Anna frowns, amused. »I rather think not. Everyone knows those beasts died out several million years ago. Just like all the other stuff around here. Everything's been dead since forever.«

»Thank goodness,« says Dina. She takes a step backwards and bumps into the turtle. »Aaargh!«

»Attention please, girls and boys!« calls Frau Lindmann. She is standing next to Mr Brownstone at the foot of a wide stone staircase which leads to the upper galleries. »I'm going to hand out the exercise sheets for the museum quiz. Please stay in your groups. We'll meet at twelve sharp in the Egyptian Collection on the second floor!«

»How very **appropriate**,« Phillip whispers to the others. »I hope we'll be able to spot the Dragon amongst all the mummies and stuffed creatures!«

Conni and the others giggle to themselves. Then they set off in their little groups to collect the **quiz sheets**.

»A museum quiz,« says Billi. »That's brilliant!«

»Well, I'm not so sure –« Conni casts a look at the sheet. »They're pretty tricky questions.«

»And there are loads of them,« says Anna. »There are some on the back, too!«

»I'm sure we'll manage it,« says Mandy cheerfully. »Wir werden das schaffen together!«

»Okay, then off we go!« Billi **takes the lead**. »Let's start with the dinosaurs.«

---

appropriate – angemessen, passend
quiz sheet – Fragebogen
to take the lead – die Führung übernehmen

A short while later, Conni is standing by a fossil of a small pterosaur, trying to find five defining characteristics of the **extinct** creature.

»He's got wings,« Mandy says.

»Wings,« writes Conni. »Right. What else?«

»Maybe his beak?« Louise suggests.

»What's a ›beak‹?« Conni puts her pen down.

»Schnabel,« Billi replies like a shot.

»Look at his egg-head,« giggles Anna.

Conni gives her a look »So am I supposed to write that down?«

»Of course,« Anna says without a moment's hesitation. »It's a defining characteristic, isn't it?«

»Odd-shaped head,« Conni writes. »That was number three. There are still two missing.«

»His claws,« says Alisha.

»Seine Krallen,« Billi translates.

»Number four,« murmurs Conni.

The girls stand in front of the glass case and stare at the ancient bird, fossilised for ever.

»Well, I can't see anything else,« says Anna.

Kate and Mandy shake their heads likewise.

»What about his **tail**?« says Dina. She is holding a notebook and is sketching the fossil. »Look: that long tail is pretty striking, isn't it?«

Conni bents over the sketch and compares it to the original. »Hey, your drawing is fantastic,« she says, adding the

---

extinct – ausgestorben
tail – Schwanz

extended spine to her list as the fifth defining characteristic.
»Thanks,« murmurs Dina, blushing slightly.

They continue to the stone-age tools, and then on to the jewellery and **burial** objects from the Bronze and Iron Ages. When Conni looks at her watch, she is astonished to see how quickly the time has gone. They've spent more than half an hour on their first tasks.
»We're done in this collection,« Billi declares. »Off we go to the second floor!«
The girls run up the wide stairs.
At the top, they bump into Paul, Phillip, Toby and a couple of other boys.
»Hey!« exclaims Phillip. »Where have you sprung from?«
»From the Stone Age,« laughs Conni. »How about you?«
»From the **bog**.« Paul looks mysterious and points over his shoulder. »Back there. But watch out: there are two *Leichen* there!«
»Leichen?« Conni taps her forehead meaningfully. »You're bonkers!«
The boys grin.
»You'll see,« says Paul.
»See you later,« says Phillip. »In Egypt.«

---

extended – verlängert
búrial – Begräbnis
bog – Moor

»What does ›Leichen‹ *mean?«* Mandy asks as they carry on.
»I'm not sure,« Conni muses, »but I think they're ›dead bodies‹.«
Billi nods. »**Spot on**. There are *Moorleichen* here.«
»What?« Anna stops so suddenly that she bumps into Alisha. »*Moorleichen?* No way! I've seen them on TV!« She shudders. »It was revolting! No, thanks. I'm waiting here.«
Mandy **tugs Conni's sleeve**. *»What is ›Moorleichen‹?«*
»Erm, I'm afraid I don't know that either. Sorry.« Conni shrugs her shoulders. *»Dead people out of a moor,* perhaps?«
Mandy pulls a disgusted face.
»Come on, it's cool,« says Billi, tramping onwards, unmoved. »You don't see that kind of thing every day!«
Anna folds her arms across her chest and **refuses** to carry on. »I'm staying here and waiting for you.«
»Okay, if you like.« Conni nods to her. »We'll be back in a minute.«
She follows the others to the end of the long room.
They stop in front of a narrow door. Behind it is a little room that is only very dimly lit.
»Dead bodies in the darkness …,« whispers Louise. *»It's like a* ***tomb*** *in a horror film, isn't it?«*
Conni feels goosebumps all over her. She swallows. She tries to see into the room, but it is too dark. Is that gruesome or

---

spot on – *etwa*: genau
to tug someone's sleeve – jemanden am Ärmel zupfen
to refuse – sich weigern
tomb – Gruft

what! She wishes she'd followed Anna's example and stayed outside the door.

»Come on!« Billi urges them. »What are you waiting for?«

Conni swallows. Okay, she says to herself. Billi's right: you don't see this kind of thing every day! And in any case: what can possibly happen? She **squares her shoulders** and takes a deep breath. »Here we go, then!«

Inside the room, it is almost darker than it had looked from outside.

Conni clutches her quiz sheet. To her left and right are glass walls. Behind them is something dark, something brown …

»Look at that!« whispers Louise. *»It's incredible!«*

Incredible? Conni stares fixedly ahead of her at a dimly lit map. Little red flags mark the spots where bog bodies have been found.

»Just look at that!« Billi is now whispering.

Out of the corner of her eye, Conni can see that Dina has taken out her notebook and is quickly sketching something. She wears a highly concentrated expression as her pen flies across the paper. She has narrowed her eyes so that they have become slits.

Conni finally shakes herself and turns to one side. Behind the glass window is a girl. It looks as if she is asleep – except for her unnaturally dark skin. It looks rather like old, cracked leather.

---

to square one's shoulders – die Schultern straffen
incredible – unglaublich

Next to the girl are rough fragments of a **clay pot** and a broken spear.

Conni is so fascinated that she can't take her eyes off the scene.

»Amazing, isn't it?« Billi comes to stand next to her. »She probably wasn't much older than us when she died in the bog. It says on the sign that she either got lost or **was sacrificed**.«

»Sacrificed? That's horrible!« Conni picks up their quiz sheet, but the light is too dim. »I can't make out the next question. I'm just going out into the light.«

Breathing a **sigh of relief**, she leaves the dark room. What on earth might be behind the other glass window? Conni isn't terribly keen to find out. She'd rather turn her attention to the next task: »Mark on your map the places where bog bodies were found.«

That is easy! Conni can remember where they were, and she makes two crosses on the little map. »Done!«

»Come on, folks, we can carry on now!« Billi looks around. »Where's Anna? She is supposed to be waiting for us.«

Conni and the others turn round. Anna has gone. At any rate, she isn't standing by the staircase any longer, which is where the others have left her only a few minutes ago.

»Anna!« calls Conni. The high walls make her voice echo unnaturally loudly. She **jumps**.

---

clay pot – Tongefäß
to be sacrificed – geopfert werden
sigh of relief – Seufzer der Erleichterung
to jump – *hier*: zusammenzucken

»Maybe sie ist gegangen zu die Toilette?« says Alisha.
»Yes, maybe.« Conni **takes a couple of paces**. »But where are the toilets? There's no sign anywhere.«
That's odd, she thinks. It isn't like Anna. She promised to wait.
»What now?« asks Billi.
»We'll have to look for her,« says Dina.
Alisha, Louise and Kate nod.
»Of course,« says Mandy. *»She can't just* ***vanish into thin air.«***
»No, she can't have disappeared without trace,« Conni agrees. »But if we go and look for her and she comes back in the meantime, we'll miss each another. Then we'll never find one another again.«
Billi nods thoughtfully. »Hmm, then we'd better split up … two of us stay here and wait, and the others go off and look.«
»But we're supposed to be staying together,« says Dina.
»No-one will know,« replies Billi. »The Dragon's miles away, and by the time she realises that our group has split up, we'll have long since found Anna.«
Right on cue, they hear **muffled** voices on the stairs.
»The Dragon,« groans Dina. »Oh no.«
»Rats!« curses Conni quietly.
Frau Lindmann and Mr Brownstone are making their way up the stairs side by side. Fortunately they are deep in animated conversation and barely notice the girls. Frau Lindmann

---

to take a couple of paces – ein paar Schritte gehen
to vanish into thin air – sich in Luft auflösen
muffled – gedämpft

merely nods to them, and Mr Brownstone waves cheerfully.
Conni breathes an **audible** sigh of relief when the two teachers disappear into the room with the bog bodies.
»That was close,« Billi whispers. »Come on, let's go before they notice that Anna's missing.«
At a run, they cross the hall and reach the staircase. There they stop, undecided.
»We've got no choice but to go to the Egyptians,« says Dina.
Billi agrees: »Yes, that's best. Anna knows that that's where we're supposed to meet.«
Conni hesitates, then nods. »After all, we've got to finish the quiz.« She waves her question sheet. »Otherwise we'll be last – just because of Anna!«
As she looks out of one of the high windows, she notices that the sky has clouded over. The cloud hangs grey and heavy over the old museum building. The trees are bending in the wind.
»It's going to rain,« says Dina, who's followed her **gaze**.
»It's good, dass wir sind inside,« says Mandy.
Conni jumps when she hears thunder in the distance. A storm – oh great. That is all they need!

On the way to the Egyptian display, they answer the questions about the different peoples pretty much as they run.

---

audible – hörbar
at a run – eilig
gaze – Blick

Conni is keen to find out more about the Inuits and the South American Indians, but there isn't time.
They only stop when they get to the **knights**. The questions are more tricky and, moreover, they haven't yet discussed the Middle Ages in class.
»What's a **halberd**?« Conni reads.
»A what?« asks Mandy.
»I love knights,« sighs Louise. »Kennt ihr die story of King Arthur?«
»I'm afraid we've not got time for the noble Knights of the Round Table,« says Billi. »Let's quickly answer the questions and see if Anna's in the Egyptians.«
She recoils as thunder rumbles close by.
»A halberd is a combination spear and battle-axe,« Dina breaks in. »It says so here.« She points to a little sign on a glass case.
»Brilliant! Thanks.« Conni writes it down while Billi looks over her shoulder to see the next question. »What's known as the morning star?«
»I know!« exclaims Kate. »The morning star ist eine Planet, isn't it?«
Conni and Billi both shake their heads. This is evidently not about Planet Venus, but the **mace-like weapon** in the case in front of them.
»A mediaeval attack weapon,« Conni writes. »So, that's that! Ancient Egyptians, here we come!«

---

knight – Ritter
halberd – Hellebarde
mace-like weapon – keulenartige Waffe

Half the class are already bustling around in the Egyptians hall. As a lurid flash of lightning lights up the sky whilst the thunder gives an earsplitting roll, there is an **electricity spike**, and the museum is plunged into darkness for a matter of seconds.

A couple of girls scream. Mandy clutches Conni's arm. When the lights come back on, they look at one another, shocked.

»Wow, that was scary,« Billi whispers.

Conni nods. »I bet it hit something.«

»You know the film ›A Night in the Museum‹?« asks Dina nervously. »Where everything comes alive at midnight? This is a bit like that.«

»Yes, it is!« Billi laughs. »The guard starts throwing sticks for the dinosaur skeleton to **chase**!«

»Oh, that's just a film,« Conni says **phlegmatically**. But her heart is beating rather fast. If only Anna would turn up again!

»Shouldn't we be looking at our quiz sheet?« she suggests.

»Yes, of course,« says Mandy. *»Let's have a look.«*

Kate, Louise and Alisha are leaning over a big glass case which housed a model of a pyramid.

»It's incredible, isn't it?« Kate says in awe. »Wie sie das haben geschafft without any machinery?«

»That's exactly our task,« says Conni. »List some ways in which they built the pyramids!«

---

electricity spike – Stromschwankung
to chase – jagen, verfolgen
phlegmatically – gleichmütig

»They used **tree-trunks** as wheels to move the heavy stones,« says Dina.
Conni looks into the glass case. »There are a couple of **pulleys** too, which they used to lift the boulders. They hitched them to donkeys and camels.«
»And slaves,« adds Billi. »They'd never have managed it without slaves!«
Conni notes down the key words, then she reads the final question aloud: »Firstly: what's the name of the Egyptian king with the world-famous golden mask? And secondly: where was his tomb discovered?«
»Tutenkhamun!« chorus Dina and Billi.
»Yes, that's right.« Conni grins. She has spotted a little notice. »It says here that his tomb was discovered in 1922 near Luxor by a Mr Carter.« She inserts the answers on the question sheet and puts it down. »Right, we've done.«
Dina looks at her watch. »Ten to twelve already! And Anna's still missing! **At twelve on the dot**, we'll have to tell the Dragon that we've lost her.«
»Oh no we won't.« Billi grins and points over Conni's shoulder. »Look who's here!«
Conni whirls round and drops her pen in surprise. Anna is making her way towards them, **chattering** happily and licking an ice cream – flanked by Frau Lindmann and Mr Brownstone!

---

tree-trunk – Baumstamm
pulley – Flaschenzug
at twelve on the dot – Punkt Zwölf
to chatter – plappern

»I don't believe it!« Conni bursts out.
»Hi!« calls Anna, waving cheerfully. »I've missed you!«
»We've missed you too,« Conni says grumpily.
Billi and Dina giggle.
»I fancied an ice cream,« says Anna. »And when I got back from the museum shop, you'd gone.« She looks **reproachfully** at them. »You promised to wait for me!«
»No, you promised to wait for us,« Conni points out. »But never mind. The main thing is you're here now!«
»You could at least have brought us an ice cream,« grumbles Billi.
Anna shrugs her shoulders regretfully. »I'm afraid I didn't have enough money. Do you want a lick?« She holds the ice cream out to Billi.
»No, thanks.« Billi pulls a face. »Let's go and hand in our quiz sheets. They'll be starting to mark them any minute now.«
»Didn't the Dragon **give you a rollicking** for being all on your own?« Conni asks, surprised.
»No. Not in the slightest.« Anna puts her lolly stick into the bin. »She spent the whole time flirting with Mr Brownstone. I don't think she even really saw me.«
The idea of Frau Lindmann flirting makes Conni giggle. With a grin, she hands the completed quiz sheet to the teacher. She is keen to know how they've done in the quiz.

***

---

reproachfully – vorwurfsvoll
to give someone a rollicking – von jemandem etwas zu hören kriegen

»Third – after all that,« says Billi. »Not bad, eh?«
Conni agrees. »It's a brilliant result when there are so many groups!«
The girls push their way down the aisle of the coach. They reach the back and sit down with sighs of relief.
Anna shakes her wet hair. »Why does it have to rain now?« she complains.
»It rained the whole time you were gone,« says Dina, somewhat reproachfully. »We thought you'd got lost!«
»Well, she's back now,« Conni growls **good-naturedly**.
Anna gives her a **grateful** look.
»All the same, I'll never forgive you for not bringing us an ice cream,« says Billi. »How could you be so **selfish**!«
»Here, have one of these instead.« Louise passes round a big bag of sweets. *»British toffees.«*
»Hey, are there any for us?« Paul, Phillip and Toby turn round in their seats.
Conni passes the bag of sweets on to them, seeing as she does so that Frau Lindmann and Mr Brownstone are sitting pretty close to one another, still deep in **animated** conversation. Well I never. Conni grins.
The coach sets off and she leans back and relaxes.
That was a brilliant morning, she thinks. What a pity that school isn't always that much fun.

---

good-naturedly – gutmütig
grateful – dankbar
selfish – egoistisch, selbstsüchtig
animated – lebhaft

»It was a great day, wasn't it?« Mandy says, as if she can read Conni's mind.
Conni nods. »And it's not over yet. What do you reckon to us all going swimming this afternoon? And then we can make another apple crumble. For those who missed it last time,« she adds.
»Yeah!« Paul, Phillip and Toby immediately agree.
»Oh yes!« exclaims Billi.
Dina and Anna nod excitedly.
»Great idea!« chorus Alisha, Kate and Louise.
»Okay,« says Conni. »We'll meet at the swimming pool at two, okay? Anyone who's late gets no apple crumble.« She winks at Anna.
»No worries,« Anna replies, grinning. »I'll be on time!«

Anna, Alisha, Dina, Billi, Kate and Louise are outside the swimming pool at exactly the agreed time. But there is no sign at all of the boys.
Conni and Mandy push their bikes to the stands and say hello to their friends.
»Sorry you've had to wait,« Conni says breathlessly, »but we had a slight problem with Mandy's **swimsuit**.«
»I left my swimsuit in Brighton,« Mandy grins. »Ich wusste nicht, dass es hier gibt eine Halle, um zu schwimmen.«
Conni rolls her eyes. Mandy not having brought a swimsuit is the least of her worries. Fortunately they are the same **size**, so lending her one is no problem. What is more difficult is stopping Mandy from **customising** her borrowed swimsuit in her own **unique** way with a few holes and safety pins.
»Are we going to wait for the boys, or should we just go in?« Anna asks.
»Let's go in,« Conni decides. »They'll find us.«
Right on cue, they hear a car horn hooting and a loud shout: »Hey! Wait for us!«
A cool dark blue Jaguar stops outside the swimming pool. Phillip, Toby and Paul clamber out, one after the other.

---

swimsuit – Badeanzug
size – Größe
to customise something – etwas individuell herrichten
unique – einzigartig

Phillip's father waves through the car window before rejoining the throng of traffic.
»Nice car,« Louise murmurs approvingly. *»Very British.«*
Laughing, they go inside and show their cards at the desk.
»Do they have Kartenkontrolleure hier?« asks Mandy, looking around anxiously.
Conni laughs. »No, just a **life guard**.«

A short while later they are splashing around like mad in the water. The swimming pool is practically empty. Just two lanes are roped off for swimming lessons.
When the boys suggest having a **diving competition** off the three-metre board, the girls immediately decline – except Louise, who can't resist any kind of sporting competition and who soon shows the boys that she is an unbeatable high-diver too. Like a water flea, she jumps from the three-metre board, turning the craziest **corkscrews** and pirouettes before ending with an elegant dive.
The others stay away, diving and swimming a few peaceful lengths. Mandy lies on her back, swimming slowly alongside Conni.
The red and white striped swimsuit doesn't suit her in the slightest, Conni decides, and, what's more, it **clashes with** her hair. She can't help grinning.
»What's so funny?« Mandy wants to know.

---

life guard – Rettungsschwimmer
diving competition – Tauchwettbewerb
corkscrew – *hier*: Schraube
to clash with something – *hier*: sich mit etwas (farblich) beißen

»Nothing,« Conni quickly reassures her. »I just think it's so brilliant, us all being together and having fun.«
»Me too,« says Mandy. She does a few crawl strokes, then takes a deep breath and dives under Conni. **Puffing**, she re-emerges. »I only wish wir könnten bleiben ein bisschen longer in Germany.«
Conni swallows. The chlorinated water is suddenly burning her eyes. »Yes,« she says. »That truly would be *really great*!«

»It was great fun in die Schwimhalle,« says Mandy the next day. »Und wenn du kommst mich besuchen in Brighton, wir gehen together an den beach, okay?«
»Yes, that would be wonderful,« Conni says thoughtfully. She is staring at the horse calendar above her desk. Just one more day and then Mandy will be gone.
»Weißt du already, wann du wirst kommen nach Brighton mit deiner Klasse?« Mandy lies on her bed, pulling at her spiky hair. »Ich hoffe, dass du wirst kommen in the summer. Dann es ist am schönsten am Meer.«
»It's not even **definite** that we're coming at all,« says Conni. »They don't normally do school exchanges at our school until we're in Year Nine or Year Ten. You visiting us was a real ›Ausnahme‹.«
»What does ›Ausnahme‹ mean?« Mandy sits up.
»It means ›exception‹.« Connny has to laugh. She is going to miss Mandy's funny questions.

---

to puff – schnaufen
definite – fest, sicher

»Oh, I see,« Mandy says **thoughtfully**. »So ich hoffe, du und deine friends werden es schaffen, Mrs Dragon überzureden, dass ihr müsst kommen nach Great Britain unbedingt.«
»It's ›zu überreden‹, not ›überzureden‹,« Conni corrects her. She scratches Mau behind the ears. The little cat purrs like a motor.
Mandy **groans**. *»Oh, I hate it!* Warum muss Deutsch sein so schwer zu lernen?«
»Hmm, no idea,« says Conni. »I think your German's already much better. You just need to ›üben‹ a bit more, then it'll be fine.«
»What bitte schön is ›üben‹?« Mandy asks in despair.
»To practise, you ›Superhirn‹.« Conni laughs. »And before you ask what ›Superhirn‹ means: it's ›superbrain‹!«
Mandy grins. »Ah, danke schön very much!«
She stands up and goes over to the desk. She has put her collection of treasures and souvenirs in the little cardboard box that Conni has given her for this purpose. Right next to it is Conni's friendship book.
»Have you written something in it?« Conni asks, **peering** curiously over her shoulder.
»Yes, I have,« says Mandy. »Aber ich brauche noch ein gutes Foto dazu.«
»No need,« says Conni. »I've got the photo that you sent me.«

---

thoughtfully – nachdenklich
to groan – stöhnen
to peer – spähen, gucken

But Mandy shakes her head. »Nein, das ist viel zu old. Du brauchst eine new Bild von mir, wo ich sehe aus, wie ich jetzt aussehe!«

»Hmm, good point.« Conni ponders. She's taken so many photos over the past few days – there is bound to be a good one of Mandy **in amongst** them which she can stick in her friendship book. Though it will take a while to get them developed. By then, Mandy will have long since gone. Suddenly she has a much better idea. »Come on!« she exclaims.

»What's up?« asks Mandy. »Warum so quick?«

Conni **drags her along by the sleeve**. »My mum has to take a photo of us! *Zusammen!*«

»›Zusammen‹?« Mandy stumbles over the top of the stairs. »That means ›together‹. Am I right?«

»Yes, ›zusammen‹ means ›together‹.« Conni groans softly. »We'll have a photo taken of us together, Miss Superbrain!«

»Oh,« Mandy grunts. »*Yes, I see.* Das ist eine wunderschöne idea!«

Conni's mother is in the garden, watering the flowers in the big pots on the patio. »Hello, you two! Why the big hurry? What are you up to?«

»Can you take a photo of us?« Conni asks breathlessly. »Of Mandy and me?«

---

in amongst – darunter

to drag someone along by the sleeve – jemanden am Ärmel mitziehen

Mum nods. »Yes, of course I can. Do you mean right now?«

»Yes, if you don't mind. We absolutely have to have it before Mandy goes home. You can **attach** your new mobile directly to the PC, can't you, and print photos straight out?«

»Yes, fine. I understand!« Conni's mother puts the watering can down. The mobile is on the patio table. »You go and stand under the old apple tree. That will make a lovely photo.«

Conni and Mandy grin at one another and get into position. Mum takes a whole series of photos and shows them the end result on the **screen**.

»They're all lovely,« she says. »The best thing would be to print them all off **straightaway**.«

»Thank you very much, Mama Klawitter,« says Mandy. »Das ist wirklich sehr lieb von Sie.«

»No problem, Mandy,« says Mum kindly. *»You're welcome!«* She switches the computer on and attaches the mobile. »The printer switches itself on automatically. Can you manage?«

»Yes,« Conni nods. »Thanks very much!« She clicks on the **›image gallery‹** button. Mandy is sitting expectantly beside her.

When their faces appear in **close-up** on the monitor, she exclaims: *»Hey, look at that!* Two supermodels unter eine Applebaum!«

---

to attach – *hier*: anschließen
screen – *hier*: Display
straightaway – gleich, sofort
image gallery – Dia-Show
close-up – Großaufnahme

»Supermodels?« Conni grins. »Not in a million years! But the pictures are great. I'll print them straight off.«
»Für mich auch please,« says Mandy.
Conni prints the pictures out **in duplicate**. »This one here is nice, isn't it?« She shows Mandy one of the photos. She and Mandy are standing under the apple tree, arm in arm and smiling at one another. »That one's going in my friendship book!«
»Ja, das ist great,« says Mandy. »Leider ich hab kein Freundschaftsbuch, aber zu Hause ich werde das Foto in eine Rahmen tun und in mein Zimmer hängen.«
Not got a friendship book? Conni's eyes sparkle. That gives her an idea!

---

in duplicate – in zweifacher Ausfertigung

On the evening before the exchange students are due to leave, there is a big **farewell** party at school. Everyone is invited – parents, grandparents, brothers and sisters, and friends.

»Well, das könnte sein die perfekte Gelegenheit, um zu machen eine totally new Conni aus dir, denkst du nicht?« Mandy is sitting **cross-legged** on her bed, using a pair of nail scissors and much dedication to add a couple of additional holes to her already battered jeans.

»Today?« Conni shakes her head. »No way! I'm not making myself the ›Gespött‹ of the whole school!«

»What does ›Gespott‹ mean?« Mandy heaves the heavy dictionary onto the bed and flicks through it. With her finger nail, she points to a page. »Ah, here it is: to make a fool of someone.« She looks up and pulls a horrified face. »Oh, no! Ich werde nicht machen ein Gespott aus dir! In the Gegenteil!«

She **heedlessly** casts aside the dictionary, nail scissors and jeans and jumps off the bed. One hand on her chin, her eyebrows knitted, she paces up and down the room.

---

farewell – Abschied
cross-legged – im Schneidersitz
heedlessly – achtlos

Frowning, Conni watches her, but doesn't say anything. Suddenly Mandy stops and **clicks her fingers**.

»That's it!« she cries. »Hast du eine old Jeans? A pair of very old jeans, die du nicht mehr brauchst zum Anziehen?«

»Yes, of course I have,« says Conni. »Why?«

»You'll see,«

says Mandy. »Hol du mal die Jeans, ich mache die Rest, okay?«

Conni rummages in her wardrobe. Her old jeans have to be in there somewhere! She last had them when she was cleaning her bike; she remembers it clearly. They are already pretty old and **faded**, with a little rip in the knee and –

»Got them!« she cries triumphantly, tossing the old jeans into the air.

Mandy catches them and examines them from all angles.

»Well, they're perfect,« she murmurs. She reaches for the nail scissors and gives Conni a questioning look. »Und du bist absolutely sicher, dass du sie nicht mehr gebrauchen wirst?«

»No chance,« says Conni. »Mum was actually going to throw them away, but –«

Before she can say another word, Mandy has sunk her nail scissors into the blue denim. Quick as a flash, she doubles the size of the rip in the knee, snips with mounting enthusiasm a couple more holes in them, rips the back pockets half off, and **frays the hems**. After a couple of minutes, the jeans look as if they've been run over by a lawn mower!

---

to click one's fingers – mit den Fingern schnippen
faded – ausgebleicht
to fray the hems – die Säume ausfransen

»Versuch mal, please.« Mandy proudly holds out the **shredded garment** to Conni.
Putting on ripped jeans isn't easy, Conni discovers. She keeps getting her foot stuck in one of the countless holes, and goes stumbling around the room. Giggling, she finally falls on the bed. It is easier lying down.
Mandy, meanwhile, **ransacks** her half of the wardrobe and pulls out a black t-shirt with cut-off sleeves. It bears a neon slogan: *»Don't feed me, I'm angry!«*
Conni bursts out laughing. »Fütter mich nicht, ich bin sauer,« she translates. »If Janette sees you in that t-shirt, she's guaranteed to leave you alone!« She gets up with difficulty and twirls round. The jeans seems to consist only of holes, rips, and frays. What a weird sensation!
Mandy throws the t-shirt at her head and fishes a little box out of her rucksack.
»Safety pins,« she announces with a grin. She intently decorates Conni's worn-out jeans with a collection of **safety pins**.
»Ouch!« howls Conni as Mandy **pricks** her. »Be careful!«
»*Oops, sorry!* But wer schön sein will, muss auch ein bisschen leiden, you know?« Satisfied, Mandy surveys her handiwork from all angles. *»And now the shirt!«*
Sighing, Conni pulls the ›Don't feed me, I'm angry‹ t-shirt over her head and looks at her reflection in the window pane. She has to laugh. The t-shirt is three sizes too big.

---

shredded garment – zerfetztes Kleidungsstück
to ransack – durchstöbern
safety pin – Sicherheitsnadel
to prick – piksen

»Du siehst so great aus!« Mandy exclaims. »Nur noch ein bisschen die Haaren und so, und dann alles ist gut für die große Party!« Before Conni can protest, Mandy has already dragged her off to the bathroom and firmly shut the door.

When the pair hurries down the stairs a short while later in their socks, desperately trying not to burst out laughing, Mum is sitting at her desk in the living room, writing a letter. Dad has made himself comfortable in his arm chair and is puzzling over his sudoku.

Mandy and Conni burst into the living room together, exclaiming loudly: »Ta-da!«

Dad drops his pen with shock. »Crumbs!« he exclaims, staring at the girls in disbelief. »Is it carnival time?«

Conni can't control herself any longer, and bursts out laughing. Mandy leans against the **door jamb**, holding her stomach with laughter.

»Conni!« says Mum, horrified. »My goodness! What on earth do you look like?«

»Cool, eh?« Conni raises her arms and does a **twirl**. »Mandy has given me a bit of a re-style.«

»Yes, I can see that!« Dad swallows drily.

Mum stands up and studies Conni's outfit from all angles. The corners of her mouth **twitch** with amusement.

---

door jamb – *hier*: Türrahmen
twirl – Drehung
to twitch – zucken

Mandy has really **gone the whole hog**! Thanks to half a tube of hair gel, Conni's hair is sticking up wildly in all directions. On top of that, Mandy has used spray colour to turn individual strands bright red. Then there are the holey jeans with their safety-pin decorations, the black t-shirt and, to cap it all, a felt-tip-pen tattoo of a spider in a web on her left arm. Even Conni has trouble **recognising** herself in the bathroom mirror.

Dad clears his throat and fishes around awkwardly under the arm chair for his biro. »You're surely not going out dressed like that?«

Mandy gets there first. With a smile, she picks the pen up. »Bitte schön, Daddy.«

»Erm, yes, thanks,« huffs Dad. *»Thank you.«*

»I'll take a quick photo of you!« Mum exclaims. »We absolutely have to have a record of this!«

Conni and Mandy stand to the left and right of the arm chair and grin like mad.

»Smile and say ›cheese‹!« Mandy says encouragingly to Dad. But he manages no more than a **crooked** grin.

»Are you really going to the farewell party in that get-up?« Mum finally asks.

»No, I don't think so.« Conni shakes her head. »I just wanted to try it out.«

»It was nur für Spaß!« Mandy agrees. »Obwohl –,« she plucks at Conni's spiky hair, »du siehst echt supercool aus!«

---

to go the whole hog – Nägel mit Köpfen machen, ganze Arbeit leisten
to recognise – wiedererkennen
crooked – schief

»I'm not as brave as you,« says Conni. »Not today, at any rate. Maybe another day.«
Dad growls something. It sounds like: »Thank God!«
Conni turns round and pulls Mandy away with her. »Come on! I've got to wash my hair and get changed. And then we'll have to go, or else we'll be late for our own farewell party!«

***

»We **ought to** really have invited Herr Fuchs and the lady from the transport office for you to say goodbye to them,« Conni says a bit later on. She is sitting with the others on a **window sill** in the hall, sipping lemonade. She has exchanged her in-your-face outfit for her favourite clothes. She feels considerably more comfortable in trainers, intact jeans and a bright t-shirt, and her hair no longer looks as if she has stuck her finger in a **plug socket** in a Force 12 gale.
Mandy opens her eyes wide. *»Are you serious?«*
»No,« Conni admits. »I hope we never see either of them ever again.«
»Me too,« says Mandy.
Phillip's father, a tall, slender man with grey hair and an open smile, is setting up a stereo in a corner of the classroom. The **caretaker**, Herr Engel, is helping him to organise the wires so that nobody can trip over them.

---

ought to – sollen
window sill – Fensterbank
plug socket – Steckdose
caretaker – Hausmeister

A few boys from their class have stuck foil on the classroom windows and posters of pop stars and football players on the walls.

When Mark switches off the ceiling light, bright spots flash in time to the music. A disco ball glitters on the ceiling.

»Cool!« Anna exclaims. »It looks like a real disco!«

Arm in arm with Vicky, Ariane and Saskia in tow as always, Janette stalks past, curling up her mouth. »How do you know what a real disco looks like?« she asks spitefully. »Babies like you aren't allowed in!«

Vicky looks at Anna and the others as if they are disgusting little insects, then turns away, bored.

Anna sticks her tongue out at Janette. »So you do know, eh? So you spend every weekend in a different disco, dancing the night away? Yeah, right.«

»You can bet your life on it.« Janette tosses her long hair off her face and **flounces off** with Vicky. Ariane and Saskia whisper something. They totter off on their high heels after Janette and Vicky, trying hard not **to twist an ankle** in the process.

»Silly girls,« Mandy hisses after them.

Phillip's head appears in the door of a nearby room.

»Hey, does anyone **fancy** a match?« he says. »Paul and I have set up the table football game!«

---

to flounce off – davon stolzieren
to twist an ankle – sich den Knöchel verstauchen
to fancy something – auf etwas Lust haben

Louise immediately jumps up and disappears with them into the room. A short while later, they hear her cheering loudly and a boy cursing under his breath.
»You watch,« giggles Billi. »Now she'll be beating the boys at table football too!«
When Mandy, Kate and Alisha get up to fetch something to eat from the buffet, Conni **seizes the opportunity**. She takes Billi, Anna and Dina aside.
»Listen,« she whispers. »I've got a plan!«
They put their heads together as Conni tells them the surprise that she's dreamed up for the following morning.
»Brilliant!« Anna says immediately.
»Let's do it!« says Billi.
»The only question is: when?« says Dina.
Conni frowns. »That's exactly the problem. We can only prepare the surprise when it's just the four of us together. If Mandy, Kate, Louise and Alisha get wind of it in advance, it won't be a surprise any more.«
»Let's go hide in the art room,« Anna suggests. »We'll have everything we need there. Maybe we could even keep the finished **items** there until tomorrow?«
Conni beams at her. »That's brilliant! We'll let Herr Engel into the secret. He'll have to unlock the room for us and make sure we're not disturbed.«
»We can collect them tomorrow morning, in good time,« says Billi. »They'll be dry by then, won't they?«

---

to seize an opportunity – eine Gelegenheit ergreifen
item – *hier*: Teil, Objekt

Dina nods. »Definitely.«
Conni holds up her hand. The others high-five her.
»Cool,« she says. »We'll call it ›Operation Goodbye‹, okay? Paul and Phillip can help us. Watch out!« She stands up. »They're coming back!«

When Mandy, Alisha and Kate come round the corner with their plates full, Conni, Anna, Dina, Billi are sitting innocently on the window sill, looking **as though butter wouldn't melt in their mouths**.
Conni stands up. »I think I'll go and get something from the buffet too,« she says, winking briefly at the others. »What do you reckon? Are you coming?«
»Sure thing,« says Anna. »Good idea!«
»I'm coming too,« Dina says quickly.
Billi rubs her stomach. »My goodness, I'm **starving**,« she murmurs. »No idea where that's suddenly come from. See you soon! We'll meet at the disco, okay?« She waves to the English girls.
Giggling, they trot round two corners and stop outside the art room door.
»I'll just run and get the key from Herr Engel.« Conni's eyes **twinkle** with excitement.
Once they've finished their work on ›Operation Goodbye‹, the buffet, run by a few mothers and fathers, has been almost

---

as though butter wouldn't melt in their mouths – als könnte sie kein Wässerchen trüben
to starve – verhungern
to twinkle – funkeln

gobbled up. But it's worth it, thinks Conni. A successful farewell surprise is more important that a full stomach!
Billi's father, Herr Verdi, has held on to the **remainder** of the pasta salad, which he gives to the four friends with a charming smile. Billi's mother adds a bit of **garlic** bread. »Hey, have you been painting?« she asks, screwing up her nose. »You smell as if you'd fallen into a **barrel of paint**.«
»Erm, yes,« Billi says quickly. »We've been painting a poster for the class disco!« She looks innocent.
»Yes, that's right,« Conni says, coming to her aid. She tugs at Billi's t-shirt and hisses to her: »I think we're arousing suspicion. Come on, let's go!«

»Where've you been?« asks Paul. He is leaning against the wall by the disco with Phillip and Toby.
Phillip raises his nose and sniffs. »Can I by any chance smell fresh paint?«
»No,« giggles Billi. »I can't smell a thing.«
»Me neither,« says Anna, an innocent look on her face. She disappears with Billi, Dina and Toby into the disco.
Phillip frowns. »What's going on here?«
Conni lets him and Paul in on the ›Operation Goodbye‹ secret.
»Cool idea,« grins Phillip.
Paul nods. »Too right!«

---

remainder – *hier*: Rest
garlic – Knoblauch
barrel of paint – Farbeimer

»So are we going to spend the whole evening standing here?« says Phillip, changing the subject. »Maybe there's something going on at the disco? Are you coming?« He gives Conni a searching look.

Conni swallows.

Phillip wants me to go to the disco with him! she thinks, horrified. I hope he doesn't want to dance with me. I'd make a complete and **utter** fool of myself!

»Erm, I'm just going to get a drink, okay?« She turns round. »I'll be back in a minute.«

Phillip **doesn't take his eyes off** her. »But don't forget,« he says. »I'll be waiting for you here.«

Conni feels as if her heart is **skipping** a couple of beats. Moreover, she can tell that her face has taken on the colour of a ripe tomato. At any rate, her cheeks are burning as if she's been **sunburnt**.

»Fine,« she croaks. »See you soon.«

Help! she thinks as she stumbles down the long corridor. Where are Anna and the others? They are never there when you really need them!

She suddenly remembers that Anna has already gone into the disco.

»Okay,« she snorts, wheeling round resolutely. »If Anna is brave enough, then so am I! It can't be that difficult!«

---

utter – völlig

to not take one's eyes of someone – jemanden nicht aus den Augen lassen

to skip – *hier*: aussetzen

to be sunburnt – einen Sonnenbrand haben

When Conni and Mandy arrive home hours later, dead tired, Mandy packs her things. She **clears out** her shelves and drawers, and stuffs everything into her gigantic travel bag.
Conni sighs. »This room's going to feel really empty without you.«
Mandy nods. She takes her souvenir box from the desk and puts it on top of her clothes. Then she hands Conni her friendship book. »Here. Ich habe etwas geschrieben für dich. I hope, du magst es.«
Cautiously, Conni opens the book and reads Mandy's entry:

Name: Mandy (Amanda) Livingston
Date of birth: 5th January
Hobbies: my dog Harry, swimming, skating, music, friends
Likes: fish and chips, Germany, ice cream with Streuseln, raspberry lip gloss, my friend Conni Klawitter
Dislikes: bus ticket inspectors, store detectives, feeling homesick
I wish you: LUCK!

---

to clear out – ausräumen

The opposite page proudly displays the photo of Conni and Mandy under the apple tree. Next to it is a little poem:

Friendship is a precious thing,
Let us shout and let us sing.
Let us stay best friends forever,
Let's forget each other never!
Your friend forever,
Mandy ☺

»Wow!« Conni says quietly. »That's fantastic! Thanks so much!«

»Ich habe es selbst geschrieben,« Mandy says **sheepishly**.

»You wrote it yourself?« Conni says, amazed. »Really?«

Mandy nods. *»I love poems and rhymes.«*

Conni quietly reads the poem out once more. Mandy moves her lips silently as she does so.

»Thank you,« Conni says again. »That's the best friendship present I've ever had!«

Conni is at once tired and wide awake. She lies on her back and stares into the darkness.

»Kannst du schlafen?« Mandy whispers.

»No,« Conni whispers back.

»Ich auch nicht« groans Mandy. »Am besten, wir bleiben wach und erzählen uns ein paar jokes.«

»Good idea,« says Conni. She stuffs her pillow behind her back, but however much she tries, she simply can't think of any jokes. »I think I'm too **miserable**.«

---

sheepishly – *hier*: verlegen
miserable – *hier*: unglücklich

»Me too.« Mandy sighs and changes the subject. »Dieser Phil … er ist ein netter boy, isn't he?«

»Yes,« says Conni. »He's really nice.« She thinks about Phillip and about the evening in the disco. They'd chatted and laughed a lot, but hadn't danced together.

Odd, she thinks. It is as if neither of them had **dared** to make the first move. She hesitates briefly before asking: »Have you ever had a **boyfriend**?«

»A boyfriend? No,« comes the quick reply. »Das kann ein bisschen warten, I think.«

Absolutely, thinks Conni, snuggling down deeper into her pillow. There really is plenty of time for that.

Next morning, Mandy and Conni are tired and silent. They've been awake half the night, chatting and crying a bit. They barely touch their breakfast.

Mandy is wearing her black t-shirt. Her **gloomy** face does justice to the »Don't feed me, I'm angry!« slogan.

As she stands up with a sigh and thanks Conni's mum for everything, Frau Klawitter **wipes** a tear away from the corner of her eye.

»Oh, I hate goodbyes,« she says, hugging Mandy. »Take care, and stay in touch, okay?«

Mandy nods, and ruffles Jakob's hair. *»See you, little one! Take care.«*

---

to dare something – sich etwas trauen
boyfriend – Freund
gloomy – düster, finster
to wipe – wischen

»Bye-bye,« Jakob says quietly.
Even he's sad, Conni thinks. She stands next to Mandy, her shoulders **drooping** and with a big **lump** in her throat. She swallows and swallows, but instead of disappearing, the lump just gets bigger.
»Are we off?« Dad is standing in the door holding the car keys.
»Yes,« Conni and Mandy say simultaneously. They look at one another and smile.

At school, Mandy says goodbye to Conni's Dad and kisses him on the cheek.
»Bye, Daddy Klarwitter,« she says. Dad grins as he heaves her bag out of the boot. »I know, I know,« he says. »You can carry it all by yourself. *You are a very strong* Mädchen.«
Mandy laughs. *»Yes, I am!«*
Once Dad has gone, Conni turns round. The others are already waiting for her.
Anna and Alisha have red eyes from crying. Billi, Kate, Dina, Paul, Louise and Toby are standing by them at the school gates, looking **awkward**.
Phillip comes up to Conni.
»Here,« he says quietly, pressing a plastic bag into her hand. »Operation Goodbye. All sorted.«
»Fantastic,« Conni whispers back. She turns and stuffs the bag into her rucksack. »Thanks!«

---

to droop – *hier*: hängen
lump – *hier*: Kloß
awkward – *hier*: betreten, verlegen

Mandy raises her eyebrows, but doesn't say anything.

They hear a loud **hooting**. Every head turns to look. Conni groans.

The red coach that is slowly making its way across the school car park is exactly the same one that the exchange students have arrived on, Conni notices. Even the coach driver is the same as ten days ago. He turns the **engine** off, opens the doors, and gets out to say hello to Frau Lindmann and Mr Brownstone. Then he opens up the luggage holds in the sides of the coach.

Here we go, thinks Conni, swallowing.

»Time to say goodbye!« calls Mr Brownstone. He energetically pushes his wheelie case into the luggage hold and claps his hands.

Conni and Mandy look at one another. Then they **hug** as tightly as they can.

»I'll miss you,« weeps Mandy.

»I'll miss you too,« sobs Conni. »*Very much* sogar! We'll write – promise?«

Mandy nods. *»And email, okay?«*

»I've got something for you.« Conni fishes a flat parcel out of her rucksack and hands it to Mandy. »Here – a goodbye present.«

»For me?« Mandy's eyes open wide.

»Yes. Open it!«

---

hooting – Hupen
engine – Motor
to hug – umarmen

Mandy **tears open** the wrapping paper. *»But that's –«*
»A friendship book,« Conni ends her sentence. »I've already written something in it.«
»My best friends.« Mandy strokes the book. *»That's so –«* Sobbing, she flings her arms round Conni. *»It's so great, thank you!«*
She opens the book. Conni has stuck two photos in: the one of them under the apple tree, and a second one that shows Dad with a forced smile, Conni on one side of him and Mandy on the other.
In her best **writing**, she has written her favourite saying:

Hast du Kummer?
Hast du Sorgen?
Soll ich dir ein Lächeln borgen?
Nimm es mit und nütz es gut,
damit es seine Wirkung tut.
Hilft es dir und bringt es Glück,
gib's mir irgendwann zurück.

Your friend from Germany:
Conni – forever!

»Thank you so much,« says Mandy, smiling. She presses the book to her chest. *»I love it. It's great!* But ich habe nichts für dich, I'm sorry.«
»Oh, that doesn't matter,« says Conni.
»Wait!« Mandy grins. »I think ich habe doch etwas!«

---

to tear something open – etwas aufreißen
writing – *hier*: Handschrift

She rummages around in her rucksack and finally pulls a rolled up piece of paper out. »Here, das ist für dich! Zum Erinnern an mich und die great time wir hatten zusammen!«
Conni carefully unrolls the paper and laughs. A black dog is grinning happily at her.
»Hey, that's the picture of Harry! Don't you want to keep it?«
»No.« Mandy shakes her head. »Ich habe ihn soon wieder in real. Please behalt es!«
»Thanks! That's fantastic!« Lost in thought, Conni studies the picture. She is thinking about the night that she'd **discovered** Mandy on the computer. Was that really only a few days ago? Almost incredible. Those fantastic days together still lay **ahead** of them then. Now, they've all gone.
»It'll get **pride of place** in my bedroom,« she promises.
»It's time to go, girls and boys!« calls Frau Lindmann. »Please load your luggage and climb aboard!«
Mandy shoulders her huge bag and pulls a face. *»I think I've got to go now.«*
»Yes, it looks that way,« sighs Conni. She smiles and gives her friend one last hug. »Take care. *See you!*«
Before they get in, Louise, Kate, Alisha and Toby say goodbye to Conni. She can see they've been crying too. They all seem to be taking the exchange students' departure very hard.

---

to discover – entdecken
ahead – vor
pride of place – Ehrenplatz

Without turning round again, Mandy **plods** to the coach with the others and flings her bag in to the open hatch to join the others there. Then she clambers onto the coach and finds herself a free window seat.

Conni, Anna, Billi and Dina are holding hands tightly. They are laughing, crying, waving and calling all at the same time.

Mandy, Louise, Kate and Alisha press their noses against the windows and wave back.

As the coach driver finally closes the doors and the coach slowly pulls away, Conni calls: »Now! Ready, steady, go: Operation Goodbye!«

She pulls the bags out of her rucksack. A poster unfurls. She quickly presses a corner of it into Anna's hands.

At the same moment, Dina, Billi and Phillip pull little flags from their pockets. As they wave with their home-made British Union Jacks, Paul holds up a German flag and waves it **to and fro** like mad.

»I've still got it from the last **World Cup**,« he grins.

Conni and Anna hold up their poster:

GOODBYE FRIENDS!

is written on it in large bright letters.

»See you soon!« Conni calls as the coach turns the corner. »We'll see you in Brighton!«

---

to plod – *hier*: trotten
to and fro – hin und her
World Cup – Weltmeisterschaft

She sees Mandy's laughing face behind one of the windows. Then the coach has gone.
They all stand dejectedly in the car park. Nobody says anything. Paul's flag hangs down **limply**. Conni and Anna lower their poster.
»So that's that, then,« Billi murmurs awkwardly.
Frau Lindmann comes over to them.
»Come on, chin up,« she says kindly. »I'm sure you'll soon see your friends again. And until then, you can phone one another and write letters. There are lots of options.«
»I wonder whether Mr Brownstone's going to write to her or ring her?« Anna whispers to the others.
»Course he will,« giggles Billi. »I bet they can't wait to see one another again.«
»That's fantastic!« grins Conni. »The sooner the Dragon manages to push through a class trip to England, the sooner we'll see the others too!«
»Pretty **ingenious**,« Phillip says approvingly.
Conni nods, satisfied. Then she turns round and starts walking slowly back towards the school. She has had a fantastic time with Mandy, and they are bound to see one another again. But now it is her old friends' turn. She **links arms** with Anna on one side and Billi on the other. Billi links arms with Dina. Side by side, they tramp up the wide steps to the school, followed by Phillip, Paul and the others.

---

limply – schlaff
ingenious – raffiniert
to link arms – sich einhaken

That's how it should always be, Conni thinks. All of us, together.
»How about going for an ice cream after school?« Anna suggests after a while.
»Great idea!« Conni smiles. *»I love ice cream with Streuseln, you know?«*

Sommer in Irland

Gesine Schulz
Eine Tüte grüner Wind
176 Seiten
Taschenbuch
ISBN 978-3-551-36252-0

Auch als englische Ausgabe erhältlich:

Gesine Schulz
The Greenest Wind
176 Seiten
Taschenbuch
ISBN 978-3-551-31883-1

Geplant war Urlaub mit Mama in den USA. Doch jetzt soll Lucy plötzlich allein nach Irland fliegen. Zu einer Tante, die sie gar nicht kennt und die in einem Haus ohne Dach lebt. Dabei regnet es auf der Insel ständig! Und außerdem haben alle Iren rote Haare. Lucy will da nicht hin, kein bisschen, aber sie hat keine Wahl. Also färbt sie sich aus Protest die Haare irisch-rot, fliegt los – und erlebt einen Sommer, wie sie ihn sich nie vorgestellt hätte!

CARLSEN

www.carlsen.de